DIGGING TO
HELL

BOOK THREE OF THE GRAVEDIGGERS SERIES
DIGGING TO HELL

WILLIE E. DALTON

All rights reserved

Copyright © 2018 Willie Dalton

No part of this book may be reproduced, distributed, transmitted in any form or by any means, or stored in a database retrieval system without the prior written permission of the author. You must not circulate this book in any format. Thank you for respecting the rights of the author.

This is a work of fiction. Any resemblance of characters to actual persons, living or dead, is purely coincidental.

Edited by Lessa Lamb
Cover & Interior Design by We Got You Covered Book Design
www.wegotyoucoveredbookdesign.com

www.authorwilliedalton.com

"Hell is empty and all the devils are here."

— William Shakespeare

CHAPTER ONE

I'M CALM NOW; THE DAYS OF FIGHTING WHERE I am are past. I've come to accept my situation. I'm not dying—the dead can't die again. I can't starve, since the dead technically don't need food, and I've adjusted to not having water. It also doesn't matter how much or how little I breathe; I can't run out of oxygen because it's all an illusion.

What I can do is plan: I can plan for the day I'm released from this coffin, and the revenge that will fall on the whole of the underworld. I will be released, be it hours, days, or years from now. He will let me out, or my friends will find me. Either way, I've learned, in life and death, that everything is temporary.

When Persephone asked me to stand in for her as queen of the underworld, I jumped at the chance. After all, who wouldn't want to be queen, even for just a little while? She made it sound so simple, and I was to have Thaddeus as my advisor in case things got complicated.

The souls that had been misplaced were being rounded up in the other afterlives after Rasputin's little game. And soon I would have my love, Raphael, back with me, and could resume serving my death sentence. However I had missed a very important detail in the otherwise simple plan: Hades.

I knew that Persephone was married to Hades, and I knew how that marriage came to be. I was educated in mythology and world religions, although I was hardly a scholar on the subject. Ray, my adoptive father, had many books from around the world that I had skimmed all throughout my life. Yet, I never asked Persephone where said husband might be, or the role he could play in the underworld. It was stupid on my part—quite possibly the most mindless thing that I've ever done. The truth was, I still couldn't comprehend that she was honest to goodness goddess, nor could I absorb the fact that even more gods and mythological beings were running around. Vampires, sure... zombies, okay—but surely Thor wasn't chilling at the local hardware store selling hammers.

But my lack of belief hadn't saved me: it didn't make him any less real, it just made me very unprepared, and left me wide open for attack.

When Hades came to see his bride before she took her annual journey to the world of the living, he was not expecting to find me... although he wasn't disappointed. He informed me of the agreement between himself and Persephone: that whoever was sitting queen while she was away was to serve as queen *in all ways*, as she herself would do.

I can still see the events playing like a movie in my mind's eye: Hades standing in front of me, untying the black robe that he wore and letting it fall to the ground. His body was chiseled in a way that you would imagine a Greek god's would be, but his olive skin had an unnatural pallor that made him look almost sickly. His hair hung nearly to his shoulders in thick black waves, and his beard was as equally impressive. At first I thought his eyes were icy blue, or even white; but when I saw my own fear reflected back at myself, I realized they were mirrors. He was an awesome sight to behold: beautiful, and terrifying.

He moved in towards me, and I couldn't seem to resist. My mind screamed at me to fight, but I reasoned that Persephone herself had lost this battle against him—*why should I even try?* I wished she had warned me.

I closed my eyes and turned my head, so I didn't have to watch myself face him as he pulled me in. He caught my face in his hand, and then his lips were on mine, forcing my mouth open to his. I summoned the strength to push him enough to say, "No."

Hades laughed a deep and haughty sound. "You can't say that to me, little one. You are my wife now, for ALL intents and purposes." He looked me up and down.

"I was not aware of this arrangement. I will turn over the crown and leave at once," I said, forcing myself to sound a little stronger.

"I'm afraid that's no longer your call to make," he said, and ran his fingers down the side of my neck. He kissed my cheek, and I shivered. "See, you respond to my touch—this won't be so bad."

I stepped back and he let me. "You are attractive, Hades, and I'm sure you are a skilled lover. But you belong to Persephone, and I am no one's to be taken without giving my consent."

He smirked at me, and nodded. "I see: a modern

woman. I've heard about those."

For a moment I thought we were going to come to an understanding, and I smiled back at him.

He stepped forward and all humor was gone from his face. "The modern ways are not MY ways, and I rule here." He grabbed my wrist so hard that I heard something pop, and I screamed.

He was pulling me towards him, despite my pitious noises, and then I heard growling… lots of growling—deep vicious sounds, like a pack of wolves had just entered the room.

I couldn't recall seeing animals in the underworld since I had been here. I forced one eye open, not sure if my situation could get any worse, and saw a huge, black, three-headed dog standing in the doorway. Its glossy ebony fur shone in the light, and all of the heads were showing teeth and snarling.

"Cerberus!" Hades called. "What is wrong with you?"

The dog growled and barked; the fur on the back of all three necks stood straight up as the dog readied itself to attack.

Hades glared down at me and my arm in his grip. I was silent now, but tears from the pain were still falling from my eyes. He seemed as confused as me about which one of us the dog wanted to attack.

The dog was suddenly closer to us, yet in the same position he had been in in the doorway, still growling, with long trails of drool hanging down the sides of its mouths. Only now the dog's eyes were locked on Hades.

"What is wrong with you, Cerberus?" Hades asked again; this time his voice was softer. "You have never turned on me in such a way. You are loyal to me, my dearest friend."

The dog stopped snarling, and then one head whimpered at his master, looked at me, and back to Hades.

"Why is it important to you that I not harm the girl? She is in my land under my rules. I can do with her as I wish." He tightened his grip once more, and another cry of pain escaped my lips.

The dog jerked its heads to me once more and narrowed its eyes; this time a small growl trickled from its lips.

Hades looked completely baffled. "Dear friend," he said to the dog, "if you feel this strongly about it there must be a reason. I will not harm her."

My heart jumped in my chest, and I wanted to run to the great beast that had saved me and throw my arms around it—I'd always been a dog person anyway.

"However, I can't let her go unpunished," Hades finished. He looked to the dog. "If she will not submit to my rules, she is to be entombed until she comes to our way of doing things."

I was hoping Cerberus would eat him. Instead, I was suddenly in the arms of two other men, being escorted out of the palace, and dragged through the underworld.

I remember entering an area that I had never seen before. There were spirits roaming, hovering just above the ground. Their faces were death-masks, with sunken cheeks, and their hollow eyes filled with desperation when they stared at—or maybe it was through—me. They frightened me, and that's when I closed my eyes. I only opened them once more when

Hades spoke to me.

"Helena, this can end whenever you want. All you need to do is call out to me and I will release you."

The room I was in was cold and damp, with only a sliver of light shining in from high above. His eyes cast my reflection back at me, and I could see myself lying in a stone coffin. I knew what the terms of my release would be, and I would be lying to say I didn't consider it, but I said nothing.

I heard the sound of the top sliding into place: the grinding noise of stone against stone—the darkness growing darker, inch by inch. I remained silent and stoic, even as the tiniest gap closed.

When I was certain they had all left the room, I gasped for air and clawed at the stone until my already short nails were bloody—and I screamed.

CHAPTER TWO

I knew my best friend Grace would get suspicious if she didn't hear from me. She had known Boude was missing almost instantly when Rasputin had left him on the other side of the wall. Maybe she would get Boude and Andreas to help her search. My mind flickered to Soren and Billy, and I wondered if she would go to them for help as well.

Soren's wife, Eira, was one of the souls Thaddeus was planning to bring back. If he had already returned with her, I didn't know if Soren would still be willing to help me—or even if he would still be in the fields where Grace could find him. Soren had been my boss, my friend, and my lover. He was my own Viking, big and strong, right down to his blonde beard and icy steel eyes. Soren had been my savior here in this new world—I had loved him, and he had loved me. It was an honor to be the first woman he had loved since death had parted him from his wife. But when the soul files were located and his wife was found, along with that of my Raphael, we knew our time was up. I couldn't believe he wouldn't still help me if he knew I was in danger, but I also didn't want to wait for a knight in shining armor who wouldn't come.

If Grace went to the other vampires, Boude and Andreas, they would likely help out of obligation, since I had helped them before. But I wasn't sure how many stones they would turn over before giving up.

No, I couldn't count on anyone finding me. As angry as I was with Persephone for leaving me here without so much as a hint to Hades's wrath, I did have hope that she would find and release me when she returned from the above world. But all of these scenarios relied on others, and I just wasn't OK with that.

Ray's voice played in my head: "Hel, above everything, make sure you can count on yourself."

Ray had raised me to be fiercely self-reliant. He would be disappointed in me if I were to just lie here and not take some kind of action—though currently I was at a loss for what exactly I should be doing. I had pushed against the top of the tomb for hours, and it hadn't budged. I had pushed against all sides of the stone coffin, and nothing moved even a millimeter. I had screamed for help, and not a single soul had answered. What was left to do?

I tried to think about what I had on my person, maybe in my pockets, or a hair pin in my hair. I tried to recall every T.V. show I had watched where someone had escaped a situation like the one I was in. Nothing was quite like my situation; I didn't remember a show where someone was entombed by the god of the underworld somewhere in his basement.

The sound of the top sliding into place echoed through my head once more, and a thought occurred to me. *Maybe I shouldn't be pushing against it, but trying to slide it back down.*

I put my hands against the top of the rough stone, and had just enough room to put my feet in the same position. The stone was rough against the soles of my feet, and I wished they had left my workboots on me. It was hard to make the sliding movement without pushing up too much on the top. It needed to be steady, even pressure that slid straight back. After each try, I made adjustments to my position to try to get better leverage. On my twelfth attempt, I felt it move.

It was only the tiniest of movements. There was no visible change, but I felt it move, and if I could do it once, I could do it again.

I tried until my arms burned and legs cramped. The palms of my hands were torn from pressing into the the rough stone, but that was OK. I could rest and try again. I had made it move, and I had all the time in the world to work on it.

I smiled to myself. I was going to get myself out of this box, and now I could rest a little easier. I closed my eyes and drifted in and out of consciousness, imagining the Hell I was going to stir up when I got out of here.

For every hundred tries, the lid moved a fraction of an inch. My palms and feet felt like raw meat, but I had light now—just a sliver: a shining glimmer of hope in all of the darkness.

I had no idea how much time was passing, or any of the events that had transpired since I had been entombed. *Is Hades ruling the underworld? Are my friends trying to find me, or do they even know yet that I'm missing?*

I wondered if Thaddeus was back with the souls, with Raphael and Eira. *Surely when he sees that I'm not in the palace, he'll go to Persephone. How are Soren—and Billy?* I missed my friends and their company, even the beautiful, egotistical, golden-haired vampire, Andreas.

My hands were sticky with drying blood, as I wiggled my fingers and clenched and unclenched my fists to try to keep them flexible. They ached with the movement, but it wasn't unbearable. It was surprising what you could endure when you knew you couldn't die or develop a lethal infection.

More time, more tries. The lid was just past eye level. I could look straight up and slightly behind me, though the sides of the coffin were too high to look far to the left or right. I was excited. The ceiling was so tall I couldn't be sure if I was looking at it, or just the shadow. The stream of light I had seen was from a small window, up so high that no one would consider scaling the slick walls to try to escape.

Once I had been able to get my fingers around the edge of the lid, I knew the work would go much faster, and it did, by comparison. But it was still damn heavy, and I still couldn't get very far with each try. I smiled at the thought of being able to sit up soon, though. It really was the little things.

With the next attempts, I was able to get the lid down past my nose. It felt like the track the top was on was more worn there, and it slid easily for second or two... until it didn't. Even though my luck was short-lived, I was grateful to raise my head and breathe in the cool damp air from the room.

I sighed with relief and let out a small giggle. Then I told myself how well I was doing, since most people in solitary confinement go a little mad—then I realized I was basically having a full-on conversation with myself, and promptly shut up.

I almost laughed at myself again: maybe I was going mad, and just didn't realize it. *What if I was dreaming everything up until this point, and this is death? This coffin... this room... What if I managed to free myself, only to wake up in it once more, over and over.* I really was losing it.

I had just started trying to push the top back further, when I heard something.

Up until now the only sounds I had heard were the ones I had made. My screams, my scratches, my crying and half-crazed laughter had been the only disturbances to echo from these walls.

My body froze and my breathing stopped. My heart pounded, and I didn't think my sense of hearing had ever been so sharp.

Footsteps. I was definitely hearing footsteps making their way towards this room. Voices—loud voices that I didn't recognize… the one doing the most talking was female. There was one, possibly two, other people in the group (judging from the voices that I heard), but strangely only the footfalls of one person.

I struggled with whether or not I should try to close the lid back over my tomb. That would mean undoing all of my hard work—and I wasn't even sure I could, on such short notice. The thought of doing all of that again made me nauseous. However if someone came in here and saw that I was trying to escape, I didn't know what kind of punishment I would be in for—

and this time, the dog might not be able to save me.

I heard the heavy door open and the sound the people walking inside. Time was up; the lid was staying open. *Shit*.

I kept waiting to see a face looking over the side of the coffin, or for someone to simply slide the top back into place—or a voice saying my name... But the female voice only spoke to her companions.

"When we go through that door, we need to be fast and thorough. Open the gates, and get out of the way," she ordered. Her voice was was distinctly female, and had an Australian accent.

I heard the eerie creaking sound of another door opening, and then the footsteps and voices were distant once more. They hadn't been looking for me.

Only a few moments passed before I heard yelling, from so many voices in so many directions I couldn't even focus on my own thoughts. Panic gripped me as I saw shadows rush by in my periphery.

The sound of running, solid footsteps of boots against the stone and dirt floor echoed nearby, mixed in with the yelling.

"What's going on? Don't leave me here!" I yelled and begged, not sure whether or not it was a good decision, since I had no idea what was going on.

The running feet stopped, and I risked it again. "Hello," I said a little more timidly this time.

A young woman, who looked to be about my age, peeked over the edge of the coffin. Her hair was longer on top and cut short around her ears. Her features were small and sharp, with the exception of her large doe-like eyes with black irises. She was exactly what I would have imagined a pixie to look like.

Her hands were perched on the side of my coffin, and at first I thought she had on a pair of black gloves. Then I realized the skin on her hands was black, and slowly blended into the ink of her heavily tattooed arms. The contrast of the black skin and ink, along with the bright colors, all against her alabaster skin, was just mesmerising.

She narrowed her eyes at me and pursed her small lips. "Who are you?"

I recognized the voice I had heard a short time earlier. "I'm Hel, Helena. Hades locked me away down here because I wouldn't have sex with him. Persephone left me in charge while she was away, and I didn't know I was supposed to…" I trailed off, and caught myself sniffing back tears.

The pixie girl huffed, and brushed a strand of hair back from her eyes with a delicate black finger. "Ugh, you wait until mum hears about this," she said.

She gave a signal to whoever was beside her, and suddenly the lid of the coffin was sliding off of me.

She offered me her hand and helped me sit up. I saw that the lid had been removed by two ghosts standing on either side of the coffin. They looked almost like translucent statues hovering just above the floor.

"Thank you," I said, trying to convey as much gratitude as possible in those two words.

"Anytime," she winked, and held my hand in hers until I was out of the coffin and on my feet.

I was so happy to be released that it took me a moment to notice all of the spirits still whizzing by in shadowed blurs.

"What's going on?" I asked.

Pixie's eyes lit up, and a sneaky smile crossed her

lips. "We opened the doors between the worlds. All the souls are running about."

"What?" I gasped. "I thought Thaddeus was negotiating all of that and bringing the souls where they need to go."

"Oh dear," she said. "How long have you been down here?"

"I have no idea," I admitted. "I don't even know where *here* is."

"Thaddeus is gone, love. No longer employed by their majesties. And 'here' is under the wall." She pointed to the doorway all of the spirits were rapidly exiting. "That is the doorway to all the other afterlives."

I was a little shocked. *Thaddeus, gone? What does that mean for the souls he was trying to track down?*

"What's going to happen now—here in this part of the underworld?" I asked.

She smiled again, and I couldn't help but notice her charm. She looked like an assassin, dressed in a tight black tank top, with black tactical pants and boots. She was both beautiful and handsome at the same time.

"Things are about to get very interesting."

"How do I get out of here?" I asked.

"You can follow me, but we have to let him know we followed orders. You wouldn't want to be a part of that."

"By him, do you mean Hades?"

She adjusted some kind of silver tool on her belt and nodded.

"You work for him?"

She chuckled, "Something like that."

"I didn't get your name before," I said. She was

walking quickly, and I was trying to keep pace—not easy after having been immobilized in a huge concrete box for who knew how long. The ghosts floated along perfectly on each side.

"I'm Melinoe," she replied without even a glance my way.

"Pleasure to meet you. So do you work for both Persephone *and* Hades?" I pressed on, trying to learn about my rescuer.

"Well, they are my mum and dad."

CHAPTER THREE

"Well he's my stepdad," she put her hand by her mouth and whispered conspiratorially, "but he doesn't acknowledge that."

"They're your parents!" I said in disbelief.

Melinoe grinned. "Indeed, they are."

"Where did you get the accent?" I asked—leave it to my brain to ask the most unimportant questions at times.

"I tried out different ones for years, but this one stuck," she said simply.

"It suits you," I replied.

She smiled, and inclined her head to the right to indicate a turn as we walked through the underground tunnels. The ghosts went a little ahead, I supposed to make sure things were safe.

Every now and then, other spirits would come by, as the last few trickled out of the other afterlives.

I pointed to the ghosts on either side of Melinoe. "Who are they?"

"They are my guards for the day. I get new ones every day, so I don't bother learning their names."

I looked at her quizzically.

"I'm the goddess of ghosts and nightmares, love. They do my bidding in exchange for me letting them spend time in the living world. Pitiful things they are, insisting on wasting away to but a shell of what they once were, trying to hang onto a life that was only supposed to be temporary." She shrugged. "But they insist."

That was a sad existence.

The tunnels were wide and well lit. We passed many doors, some with large locks. I wanted to ask what was inside, but we passed by them so quickly, and I needed to worry about the things that were going on when I got out of here.

Above everything, I wanted to get back to the fields, or even into the Vampire Quarter. I needed to find a familiar face, let them know I was OK, and let them know what was happening.

"Does your mother know what's going on?" I couldn't believe that Persephone would just stand idly by as Hades turned the underworld she had created into this chaotic place.

"No, and I'm afraid I can't reach her at the moment. With Thaddeus no longer running messages back and forth, she is unaware and thinks things are fine. He is the only one who knows where to find her in the above world."

"So she doesn't even know that Thaddeus has been fired? How can Hades do that, since Thaddeus was her advisor?" I asked.

"When the god of all the underworld tells you you're fired, it's not something up for debate," she said sternly.

Having met him, I could certainly understand that.

"So we just have to ride all of this out until it's settled, or she comes back and tries to reason with him?"

"Pretty much," Melinoe said as she bounced up a stairway we had come to.

I could see light pouring in at the top of the stairway, and knew it had to be the entrance back into Persephone's palace. I was not looking forward to going in there, even if it meant finding a way out.

As if she read my mind, Melinoe said, "Wait here at the top of the stairs: let us see where he is, and I'll send one of my guards to lead you out another way."

I nodded in understanding. As she turned to leave the doorway, I touched her shoulder. "Thank you again for helping me."

She traced a finger down the side of my face and winked at me.

I waited in silence as she and her guards went to find Hades. Just the thought of possibly bumping into him ever again made my stomach hurt. I recalled the vampire Rasputin, and how his very presence had repulsed me with the evil he exuded.

The reaction I had to Hades was different. I was frightened of him and the power he had, but I knew underneath that there was some level of attraction: a drawing energy that he possessed. He wasn't evil, he just *was*, with no thought to good or evil, only "his way." That indifference was intriguing, and very dangerous.

Melinoe's ghost guard came back more quickly than I had expected. The pale hand motioned me, and I followed. I found myself creeping through the lush indoor garden, where I had watched Persephone tend to her flowers.

Tall green trees stood above me, their branches heavy with colorful fruit. Water flowed from the mouth of a silver ram's head into the pond, and the sound of it rushing out played like white noise as we walked through.

Once at the exit, it felt almost too good to be true that I was going to be able to walk out of here—to leave this palace that had become my prison.

I thanked the ghost for escorting me to safety, and received a bow from him in return. I pushed open the heavy glass door and stepped out into the underworld that I had come to call home.

I'd had a feeling things were not how I had left them, and I was right. Spirits roamed the streets, and nothing looked the same.

The streets were dirty, and people were everywhere. I heard crying and screaming, and couldn't figure out what was going on. I didn't feel scared—I didn't feel anything, really. I wanted to check on my friends, and after that, I wasn't sure.

I made my way back to the streets that were more familiar to me, as I ducked and dodged the people that were crowding and rushing by. I noticed that the floating spirits were starting to become more solid as they moved around. I even watched as a few went from silently hovering, to taking firm steps on the sidewalk.

Andreas's boutique was on my way, so I ran in, hoping to find him or Grace. But when I went inside and called out, no one answered. I walked through the racks of clothes and looked in the back. I'd never seen the store empty—there are no "business hours" in the underworld. Someone should be here. Things were very wrong.

I considered going into the Vampire Quarter to look for them, but my heart just wanted to get back to the fields where I could see Soren and Billy. I wondered what was happening with the dead right now.

Recalling Rasputin once again, I shivered, remembering how the zombies he had created had clawed themselves out of the graves. *Are they doing that now?*

I had been able to help when the underworld was in danger from one madman, but this was something entirely different. This was *gods and goddesses*. I hadn't even considered how I might help, unless I could figure out a way to get in touch with Persephone—and her daughter, Melinoe, had made that sound impossible.

The familiar path back to the fields of the dead didn't feel very familiar right now. The energy was so different, it was like another world. Normally, the underworld was calm, with everyone doing their own thing and leaving everyone else alone. The streets I passed by were slowly looking more and more empty, with the few people I saw appearing to be in a terrified frenzy.

The brown and gray fields appeared in my line of sight, and I took off running towards them. I couldn't wait to jump into Soren's arms, even for just a moment, to feel something I loved.

As I approached the barren land, I realized it was just that: barren. There were no reapers out digging. I told myself maybe they were just inside resting, but I knew that wasn't the case. It felt different… empty.

I walked out into the brown fields of dirt and looked

down, using my bare foot to move some of the dirt, to see the little silver tags that mark the names of the people in the graves. The tag was there, but there was no name. I moved down the row, and tag after tag was blank.

That's why there were no reapers: right now, there were no dead people.

CHAPTER FOUR

I RAN TO THE BOXY LITTLE HOUSES ALL OF THE reapers had lived in, and resisted the urge to first go into the one that had been mine. I knew no one was there, but I did make a mental note to go in and grab some boots and fresh clothes before I headed back into town.

Soren's house was close to mine, and as I knocked on his door, my heart hurt; there was a lump in my stomach I just couldn't choke down. He had loved me, and I him. I was supposed to get my Raphael back, and he was supposed to get his wife. I needed to find him, to see if they were together, to make sure at least one of us was happy. And if not, then dammit, I wanted him back.

No answer. I turned the knob and found the door was locked. I sighed. I was glad it was locked. That meant he had taken the time to lock it, and hadn't left in such a hurry as to leave everything wide open.

I went to Billy's door next, and found it the same as Soren's. Of course Billy wouldn't be home, though. If anything was wrong, he would have rushed into town to see Margaret, his girlfriend.

Back at my own house, I crossed my fingers and lifted up the mat in front of my door to see if my key was still there. When I went to stay at the palace, I wanted to leave my key behind, in case I needed one of my friends to bring me something. I had packed a lot, but not everything. It was there.

Once inside, I tried not to look around—to stay focused, and not let the memories hit me. I didn't want to see the bed where Soren and I had made love so many times, or any of the little things that might trigger tears.

I wanted a shower, but there wasn't time for that. I threw on a clean t-shirt, with jeans, and my extra pair of boots. My hair went up in messy bun, and that was as good as things were going to get.

Outside, I resisted the urge to go to the shed and get my shovel and tools to dig in the fields. I missed working. Digging was all I knew, and I craved that routine.

Instead, I headed back towards the city.

My first stop was the Assignment Hall. As I walked inside the plain looking building, with the too-ornate pearly doors, I wished that I had happier memories of this place. It was the first stop for everyone once they woke up from the grave. It was where you got assigned your job, and where you checked in to see how much time you had left to work off before your soul was settled.

The first time I was here and assigned as a reaper, I was still freaking out about being dead. The second time, when I came to check in after working five-hundred hours, was when I discovered it had been taken over by vampires. And the last time was when

Grace had handed me the files that said where Raphael and Eira were. Maybe the last one should have been happy… but it was too jarring.

I half expected the Assignment Hall to be as deserted as everywhere else in town, but to my surprise, everyone must have had the same idea as me. Crowds of people and half formed spirits were lined up by the office doors and desks. It did make sense: people liked to know what they were supposed to do—what was expected of them.

If I went into a new afterlife that I knew nothing about, my first stop would certainly be the place where new souls got assigned.

I stepped into a corner beside a potted plant, out of the way, so that I could watch the goings on and figure out where I should be. I touched the leaves of the plant, not sure if I expected it to be real or fake. It was real, and I recalled all of the lush greenery back at Persephone's palace. I shivered a bit, and moved so that the wide leaf no longer touched my arm.

Every now and then, a new person would come inside and choose a line to stand in at random. I was surprised at how calm everyone seemed to be. The hall was filled with the sounds of people talking to one another, but no one was screaming or yelling, and no one was smiling or laughing either.

I snaked my way in and out of lines, looking for a familiar face, and found myself at the door that I knew led to the basement. Maybe Margaret would be down there working, and I could find out where my friends were.

I had just pushed the door open and started to step down when I heard my name called.

"Hel? Is that you?"

I froze. I knew that voice—I'd have known it anywhere, even whispered through a crowd of thousands of people. Of all the people I could have found, I never expected to find him.

He said it again, "Helena," and this time he was closer.

I felt the heat from my tears as they poured down my face like a faucet had been turned on. Slowly, I turned around and clapped my hand over my mouth to choke back a sob. It was him: the only dad I had ever known. It was Ray.

He watched all of the emotion wash over me, and I saw the tears falling from his own eyes. I ran to him and grabbed him in the tightest hug I've ever given anyone.

We cried on each other for a long while, and finally, he was the first one to pull back.

He took my face in his hands and searched it. "My girl," he said. "What happened? You should still be home and living your life." He said it with so much sadness in his voice that it hurt my heart.

"It's a long story," I sniffed, not wanting to elaborate. "I've been here a while—how am I just finding you?"

"I just got here. I was in another area, sorting through my last life and deciding when and where I was going to go back. A big door opened up in the wall and everyone started going through it, thinking they were supposed to. Once I realized what happened, I was stuck here." He smiled at me. "But now, I'm so glad it happened."

"I'm so happy to see you." I leaned forward and kissed him on the cheek. He looked like he did before he got sick, before he died. He was still older, with white hair, and skin permanently dark and aged from all the years digging in the sun. His blue-green eyes sparkled at me, and the sound of his raspy voice comforted me like a baby being held by it's momma. He was my momma: my momma, and my daddy, and for the better part of my life, he was my best friend. I just couldn't imagine how people lived without a Ray.

I tried not to get too caught up in my sentiments. "Do you have any idea what they're going to do with everyone? Will you be able to get back?"

He shrugged, and it was a strong movement; I watched as the muscles in his shoulders moved.

"I have no, idea," he admitted. "Do you know anything about any of this?" he asked me.

I couldn't really say no, but I didn't know enough to be helpful. "Eh, it's some deep shit. I'm trying to learn more."

Ray looked a little uneasy at my answer, and I couldn't say that I blamed him.

"I'm looking for some friends that might have answers. Do you want to come with me, or do you think you should stay in line and see if you can get answers that way?" I asked.

"You go on, I'll stay here. That makes the most sense," he said.

I hesitated to turn and walk away from him, and he noticed.

"I'll wait up here for you, right by that door, if I finish before you. I'm not going to leave you," he said as though he was reading my mind.

It felt like the first day of school all over again. I was no longer the Hel who had been on her own for years, alive and dead: the one who had run her own cemetery, and fought off evil vampires. I was a nervous little girl with blonde hair, afraid to leave the safety of the person I knew was always watching out for me.

I gave Ray my most confident smile and nod, and headed down to the basement.

Relief washed over me as I reached the bottom step, and was met with a chorus of friends shouting my name.

Grace, of course, was the first one to practically jump into my arms and kiss me on the lips, which made me laugh out loud. Then, I was being hugged from behind by Boude, while his ruby hair enveloped us all in the scent of blood and exotic spices. The lights danced in the cut emeralds that were his eyes, and I was so grateful to see my sweet friends.

"Stop being greedy," I heard Andreas say.

I pulled away from Boude and Grace, and moved as they stepped into each other's arms. I turned to Andreas, who surprised me by pulling me into another tight grip, and petted my head—like I was a cat struggling to get away from my obsessive owner.

Andreas wore a cream colored shirt with a v-neck over halfway down his chest, and a pair of brown corduroy bell-bottoms (his trademark); his golden mane of hair was as lovely as ever, and his pupil-less honey eyes were full of spirit. He and Boude were the most colorful, and beautiful, vampires I had ever seen, and I'd seen quite a few at this point.

Finally, I pushed away from Andreas's fervent attentions. "Glad you missed me," I said as I tried to smooth down the fly-aways in my now-even-messier bun.

"You had better have the best fucking story about where you've been and why we haven't been able to find you." His hand on his hip as he scolded me added extra sassiness to the words.

I was about to say that I did indeed have the "best fucking story," but I heard a sweeter voice say my name, and knew it belonged to my friend and fellow reaper, Billy.

"Billy!" I exclaimed, and gave him a hug, as well as his girlfriend Margaret.

"We tried to find you, Hel. We looked and looked, and—"

I cut him off. "It's ok, I knew you were trying—all of you." My eyes scanned the room; I didn't want anyone feeling they had let me down. And then my eyes landed on someone I didn't even realize was in the room… Soren.

Soren is a big guy: we're talking take-up-a-doorway-with-his-muscles kind of big. I didn't call him my Viking for nothing. So for me to have missed seeing him in this little basement room, I knew he had wanted it that way; he was hiding from me. A quick look to his left told me why. Standing by his side was a woman. I knew with full certainty that woman was his wife, Eira.

CHAPTER FIVE

I didn't know what Soren had told her about me, if anything. I was terrified to do or say the wrong thing, and I was crushed that I couldn't run and jump into his arms and kiss him.

He saw me looking at him, and the look he gave me was as cold as the the first time he met me—when he had dug me up in the fields, and I'd started sobbing.

I swallowed hard and straightened my shoulders, walking over to him. "Hello, Soren."

"I am glad you have safely returned. I've missed working alongside you in the fields," Soren replied. There wasn't a trace of emotion in his words.

I lowered my gaze for a moment to smile, before looking back up at him. "Thank you. I've missed the company in the fields as well."

Eira stood beside Soren. She was shorter than I expected her to be, barely five feet tall. Her light blonde hair hung to her waist, and her eyes were a pale blue that reminded you of crystal glaciers. She looked older than I expected, as well: the lines around her eyes were fairly deep, and the skin on her neck wasn't as firm as it once was. I remembered that this was at least her second pass through death, and wondered what her last life had been like. It wasn't my business to know, just plain old curiosity.

Eira glanced at Soren, and I gave him the same look. It was an "Aren't you going to introduce us?" kind of look. He pretended he didn't know what it was about.

Eira held her hand out to me. "I'm Eira, Soren's... wife." She hesitated as she said the word "wife," and I immediately wanted to know what was going on between them.

I shook her hand. "Helena, Hel for short. Pleasure to meet you."

Soren looked uncomfortable.

Andreas cleared his throat. "Hel, we are still waiting for you to tell us where the Hell you've been, and what the fuck is going on."

I turned back to him and nodded. "You're right. First, I need to run upstairs and get someone."

Grace hugged Ray almost as tightly as I had. "I have heard sooo much about you!" she gushed.

Ray smiled, and hugged her back like he had known her all of her life. He didn't bat an eye while meeting my vampire friends, even though he said there weren't any vampires where we was previously.

I couldn't get over being reunited with Ray, although I still couldn't shake the helpless-little-girl feeling I had being around him.

After introductions were made, everyone sat down and got quiet for me to tell the story of what had happened to me. I didn't want to tell it, especially the part about Hades expecting to have his way with me, but I did. I told the whole story, and afterwards everyone was shocked and silent.

I looked to Ray first. His brow was furrowed so hard it made me rub my own; his fists were clenched in his lap. I'd rarely seen him angry in life, but I knew these were the key signs for him.

I put my hand on his knee. "I'm OK," I said.

His expression softened as he gazed at me, and he shook his head with a look of defeat.

"So let me get this straight," Boude said. "Persephone can't be reached, and Thaddeus is not at liberty to give her whereabouts; Hades is currently ruling, and the doors to all the afterlives have been opened, so we have no idea which souls go where?"

"Basically," I replied.

"Oh dear," Boude said, and bit the side of his lip. "You realize what this means, right?"

"Yeah, it means it's a big mess, and I don't know how we're going to sort out any of the souls," I sighed.

Boude shook his head with a little more force than usual. "No, I mean, the gods of the other realms are going to come here to reclaim the souls that belong to them, and they won't be happy."

The realization of that fell over all of us like a blanket of snow—heavy, cold, and silent.

"What can we do?" I asked, not feeling very hopeful.

"This one is out of our hands, I'm afraid. This was Hades's doing: the work of a god. There isn't one here among us who can take on him, or anyone of his nature. The best we can hope for is to find out what his next moves are, so we can try to get out of everyone's way," Boude said.

We all seemed to agree.

"Do you think you could find Melinoe again? Ask her if she could keep us in the loop about what's going on?" Ray asked.

"I'm a little afraid to go back towards the palace, but yes, I'll see if I can find her," I said.

I turned to Billy and Soren. "What's going on in the fields? All the name plates were blank."

"There's no one to dig up—the graves are empty," Billy said with a shrug.

Wide-eyed, I turned to look at Soren.

"People aren't dying," he said cooly.

"That can't be good," I said.

"We're safe, right?" Andreas asked, pointing to himself, then Boude and Grace. "I mean the vampires. We should be safe—we don't have souls, so we're not involved in this?"

"Some of these gods could blink us out of existence. We're no use to them without souls, so they might not bother keeping us around," Boude lectured.

Andreas looked a little pale, and didn't have a comeback.

"Where is a safe place for all of us to stay in the meantime? I'm a little scared," Margaret's voice was a bit higher than usual, with an edge of panic. Billy put his arm around her and gave her a reassuring squeeze, but she didn't seem to relax into him.

"That's a good question," Ray agreed. "Is there a place we can all stay together? It might not be totally safe, but at least we can try to keep track of one another."

"The houses in the fields are right in the open, and not big enough for all of us," Billy answered, and I heard Soren grunt in agreement.

"Our apartments aren't big enough either," Grace said, speaking for the three vampires.

I had an idea, but I didn't like it. "Is anyone living in Rasputin's old mansion?"

All the eyes in the room fell on me.

Boude smiled. "Brilliant idea! No, no one is there. It might be a little dusty, but otherwise can house us all nicely."

Great...

I caught a glimpse of Eira tugging on Soren's arm and whispering something into his ear. Her face didn't look too happy.

For a moment, I remembered licking and nibbling on that ear the last time we were together. The moment gave me a petty spark of joy. *What is wrong with me? I wanted this for him,* I argued with myself. *Then again, I also believed I was getting Raphael back when he got her back.* My moment of jealousy justified, I tried to move on. Apparently the conversation had continued without me.

I heard Grace say, "So it's agreed we'll all stay together, go by each other's homes to pick things up, and onto the mansion in the Quarter, so none of us get seperated?"

Everyone nodded in agreement, except for Soren and Eira. She was not happy with arrangement, I could tell. I wondered if Soren had told her about us, or maybe she just didn't like vampires. Other than the three in the room with us, I didn't care for them either.

CHAPTER SIX

The line hadn't budged, even by the time we left. People were starting to get anxious and meander about, so luckily we weren't noticed when we quietly snuck out the back door of the Assignment Hall.

Margaret's place was closest, so the rest of us waited outside as she and Billy ran in for her to grab some things. She was more scared than I had seen her before, so she was in and out in a flash.

Next, we went to the fields. Knowing all of that land was bare, above and below, felt strange—it felt sad. How weird was it that I found it *sadder* that there were no bodies to dig up, no souls to reap, no death in the living world. *Shouldn't that be a happy thing?* But the emptiness made me feel useless. Digging was all I knew, on one side of the grave or the other.

Ray walked along beside me, and I longed to show him how to be a reaper. He would have gotten such a kick out of it, and I had really missed digging with him.

Soren held Eira's hand as they walked through the endless brown dirt. Her eyes stayed focused straight ahead, as his wandered, like mine, through the rows and memories we had tied to this place. She didn't get it.

Billy held Margaret's hand, too, but his eyes stayed lowered to the ground, searching each little silver tag for a name. I saw him shake his head a time or two in disbelief. This was all he knew as well.

We came to my door first, and I shook my head. "I got what I needed earlier, and everything else I have I left at the palace."

Billy walked on down to his place, and Margaret went with him. "Just gonna grab some clothes," he said in his eastern Kentucky accent. His voice always made me smile, and reminded me of home in the southern Appalachian Mountains.

Eira had a tight grip on Soren's arm, and he looked downright uncomfortable. It annoyed me seeing him like this. Seeing someone exert power over one of the strongest people I'd ever met: big turnoff.

Her nails dug into his skin as she squeezed harder and looked up at him. Soren grumbled, but spoke up. "Friends, I think Eira and I are going to stay here. She feels—" I watched the nails go into his flesh again before he corrected, "We feel that it's safer to stay here, than to be in the Vampire Quarter. We understand we are taking our chances by being on our own, and if anything changes, we will come straight to the mansion," he finished.

During *his* little speech, I had crossed my arms, and now I couldn't help but to roll my eyes. It was so obviously not THEIR idea, but hers. If I truly thought that he agreed with her, maybe I wouldn't have been so annoyed by the choice.

"That's a stupid decision." I heard the words only a

milli-second before I realized I was the one who'd said them. *Oops.*

Soren looked at me with eyes that pleaded for me to shut up. Eira looked… pissed.

I wanted to turn and walk off somewhere, but didn't really have anywhere to go just yet. So I held my ground, and my gaze.

Ray looked down and shuffled his feet a little.

"It really would be much safer, for all of us if we stayed together," Boude said.

"Dude, we can't help you or her if you're all the way in the fields," Andreas added.

"We are warriors. We will not need your protection." Eira had the audacity to try to look superior, even while she stood more than a foot shorter than Andreas. Some petite people had presence, some had ego. Guess which one she had.

Soren had to look away from the scene. I watched as his cheeks reddened with embarrassment.

I had a moment to feel sorry for him; I was willing to bet the woman beside him wasn't quite the wife he remembered.

Billy was back now, and quickly caught on to the situation. He didn't even give Eira the courtesy of a passing glance. If Billy didn't like her, that told me everything I needed to know, because he was the most understanding person I had ever met (outside of Ray).

Billy just shook his head at Soren and said, "Be careful, buddy." The "be careful" held a lot more meaning than just the political stuff that was happening.

Soren said nothing, but gave Billy a weak smile. Eira stared at Billy, waiting for acknowledgement. He didn't give her an ounce.

I so wanted to know what had happened since I left, and how long she had been back.

We left Soren and Eira in the fields to fend for themselves, and made our way into the Vampire Quarter.

The gothic spires and black brick streets that had seemed so menacing to me for so long, now felt protective and welcoming. *Hmm, I never saw that coming.* I even caught myself smiling as I walked the streets and glanced in the shop windows.

The red lights in the downtown area were turned off. Guess the vampire escorts were even being cautious at the moment. I'd never seen them closed.

We all waited in Andreas's elegant red and gold living room while he packed. Naturally, he came out of his bedroom rolling two large tapestried suitcases. Somehow I knew he couldn't pack light.

Boude and Grace declined stopping at their apartment, since they had some things left at the mansion from when they stayed there previously as servants of Rasputin's.

We had all been pretty quiet as we traveled, and I couldn't help but feel like we'd lost one already, without having Soren with us.

I had forgotten how remote the mansion was: not just on the outskirts of the Quarter, but on the fringes of those skirts. As it came into view, I recalled facing Rasputin, and all the angry vampires and zombies—how it felt being carried away with Andreas and imprisoned below the old courthouse in the dungeon. At the time it was terrifying. If only I'd known a short time later I was going to be entombed under the wall,

I could have considered the prior incarceration a mini-vacation. I chuckled softly to myself—my sense of humor had gotten dark since I died.

Inside, I was once again overtaken by the luxury and light of the space: so much white marble with gold accents and brilliant chandeliers. If I hadn't had a first-hand glimpse of the atrocities committed by Rasputin, it might seem like a fun place to stay.

"Should we stay in the upstairs bedrooms?" I directed the question mainly at Boude and Grace. They agreed.

"We'll have to split up on the top two floors, but I don't think anyone wants to stay in his old bedroom," Grace said.

I had been the one to find Rasputin's bedroom when we were searching the house for the souls he had stashed away. It was dark and evil, with tapestries of tortured faces hanging on the walls, and bottles of sick and sticky fluids sitting around.

"I might," Andreas said.

Boude shook his head fervently at Andreas, and Andreas seemed to understand. "Really, that bad?"

"Rasputin's taste for depravity and debauchery was of a different nature than yours, my friend." Boude put a hand on his shoulder.

Andreas didn't mention it again.

"Let's let Hel, Ray, and Billy and Margaret, have the three bedrooms on the top floor, and the vampires on the floor below. That way if someone comes in, we are the first ones they face," Grace suggested, having worked it all out in her head.

"Excellent plan, my love," Boude cooed, and kissed her head.

I wasn't sure how much security my vampire friends could provide if gods of old came crashing through our door, but I appreciated the thought just the same.

We all headed up the grand staircase to the top two floors. It didn't feel quite as creepy up here. I assumed that was because Rasputin hadn't spent nearly as much time in this part of the house.

Ray took the bedroom across from mine, and Margaret and Billy took the one next to his.

Mine was a pretty room, with old, heavy furniture, made of a dark mahogany wood. The bedspread was a mustard yellow that wasn't overwhelming in contrast to the wood, and the golden light that glowed from the chandelier blended things together nicely.

I walked over to the window and looked down at the empty street, and out at the silhouette of the Quarter in the distance. I never imagined I would be choosing to stay in this house, though it wasn't as bad having my friends here with me. I thought of Soren and Eira back in the fields, and hoped they were OK.

"You doing alright?" The voice came from behind me in the doorway.

I turned and smiled at Ray. "I am. Just tired."

He shook his head and ran his fingers through his hair.

He had taken off the blue shirt he had on earlier, and was in a white undershirt, still wearing the same jeans and black leather belt. It reminded me of life with him back at our cabin in the cemetery, watching him fry bacon and eggs in the morning before we got to work.

"Are you alright?" I asked him.

He smiled and let out a breath. "Yeah. I couldn't be happier to see you again. I just wish the circumstances were a little different."

"A smart man once told me that nothing is ever perfect, and you just have to appreciate whatever good you have at the time," I winked at him.

"Must've been a smart feller that told you that."

"The smartest," I replied.

CHAPTER SEVEN

THE TIME ALONE IN OUR ROOMS TO REST AND regroup made all of us feel a little better, and not quite as hopeless. I knew that I needed to head back into town to try to track down Melinoe; I still wasn't very excited about that.

We were all in the large living room, where everything was way too fancy for us to feel relaxed, with the exception of Andreas, who was lounging across an elegant black chaise looking like a happy cat. He always felt at home in luxurious settings.

Boude and Grace were sitting on the edge of the couch with their arms around one another, Ray was pacing and looking out the windows, and Billy and Margaret were discussing going back to the Assignment Hall to see what they could learn.

"Should you go to the fields and check on Soren and Eira?" I asked Billy.

"He's a big boy. They know where to find us," Billy said in a tone of voice I'd never heard come out of him.

Billy was so sweet and lovable, to see him upset was foreign. Margaret put her arm around his tall, skinny frame and leaned into him. He pulled her closer and kissed her on the head, his frustration visibly easing.

"There's more to this than I know, isn't there?"

"I don't think she's the same person he knew once upon a time, or maybe it's him that changed. He's not been himself since she came back, which would be OK if he was happy. But I think he just feels obligated to make it work, since he waited so long," Billy said.

"When and how did she get back? Was is when the doors were opened, or before, when Thaddeus was gathering the souls? I mean, I don't even know how long I was gone," I rambled.

"She was one of the first souls that Thaddeus retrieved. When he told her that Soren was waiting on her, he said she couldn't wait to return to him," Boude said. "That was very soon after you left, within what would probably be a week."

I couldn't recall the details of the things that had happened in the palace before I met Hades. I knew I hadn't been there long; I didn't remember Thaddeus telling me he had retrieved any souls.

"Did he bring any others back with him?" I asked.

"A few, but not the one you're asking about," Andreas answered.

"Eira has just been difficult since she got here. She didn't want to get assigned, tried to keep Soren from reaping and encouraged him to find another job, and she made it very clear she didn't want me hanging around him. She's just tried to keep him all to herself," Billy grumbled.

"It's been a hundred years or more since she saw him, maybe she just wants some time with him to reconnect," I said, not sure why I was trying to defend her.

Billy shook his head. "I don't think that's it. Why would she avoid getting assigned, and what reasons does she have to dislike any of us?"

I didn't have any good replies, and no one else seemed to think they had anything to add.

"She has no redeeming qualities?" I asked. I knew Soren pretty well, and I found it hard to believe he would think so highly of someone unworthy.

Andreas rolled his head to look at us as he joined the conversation. "She must have a powerful pussy."

I bit my lip a little too hard, and felt my face redden. I did not want to think about Eira's pussy, on any level. I turned away, hoping no one would notice my discomfort. Andreas's eyes caught mine—of course *he* noticed, but he didn't call me out on it. I appreciated that.

"I guess I need to get out of here and find Melinoe," I sighed.

Ray walked over to me. "I don't think you should go alone. None of us should be out by ourselves."

I looked around the room, waiting for someone to offer. My eyes lingered on Grace long enough for her to get my hint.

"I'd be glad to come with you," she said, standing as she volunteered herself.

I wasn't certain she was being truthful about the "glad" part, but I was grateful.

"Thanks," I said.

Boude didn't look happy about her going with me, but didn't protest as she let go of his hand.

Grace brushed her silky, black hair behind her ear on the whole side of her face, and kissed her love on top of his head, letting her fingers play a moment in his curls. "I won't be long."

I watched as Boude closed his eyes and sighed at her touch. I hadn't approved of their relationship in the beginning: a nearly centuries old vampire with a recently dead young woman—I was sure his motives were less than pure. But in time, I had come to see the love that he had for her was indeed real. It made me happy.

Grace straightened and walked over to me. As she moved across the room, I was struck by how much older she looked, which was odd. Whatever age you died at was the age you stayed in this part of the underworld. She had killed herself at seventeen to escape a very bad person, and had chosen vampirism soon after meeting Andreas. I didn't approve of her giving up her soul, but looking at her now, it wasn't physical aging I saw, but strength, confidence, and yes, *grace*. She moved across the floor like a tiger, muscles subtly gliding just beneath the skin. No matter the situation, she always looked like a sexy assassin. Today it was a black leather vest that zipped up the front, red leggings, and black boots that laced all the way up and over the knees. She was wearing her black leather eye-patch, and her red lips matched the leggings. When I dug her up, she'd looked like a sweet little school girl, in clothes the pedophile had put her in for all of eternity. The moment she was able to make decisions for herself, she never looked back.

"What's your deal?" she asked, raising an eyebrow at me.

"What do you mean?"

"You're just staring at me, grinning kind of stupidly," she said.

""Sorry... I was just looking at how pretty you are, and thinking how far you've come. I'm really proud of you," I told her.

"Aww, Hel!" Grace said sweetly, then hit me on the arm. "Stop it! I don't want to cry off my eyeliner."

With a parting wave to everyone, we went out the door and headed in the direction of the palace. I really hoped we learned something useful, and most of all, I really hoped we got to come back.

As we walked towards town, Grace seemed more quiet than usual.

"What's on your mind?" I asked her.

"Do you hate me?" she asked.

I stopped walking and looked at her. "Why on earth would I hate you?" I was genuinely stumped.

"I don't know how long you were missing before we realized it. I just assumed you were safe, and needed time to process everything with Soren. I should have been checking on you." She wouldn't meet my eyes. "I swear though, as soon as we realized something was up, we asked everyone, and looked everywhere we possibly could. We couldn't find you."

"How did you learn I was missing?" I asked.

"Soren went to see you at the palace. It was just before Thaddeus brought Eira back. Someone he didn't recognize answered the door, and said they had no idea who you were and pretty much dismissed him. Then we all went back, and the same thing happened. It was so awful, and they wouldn't let us in to look for you." A tear streamed down from Grace's amber colored eye.

I hugged her tightly, and she cried on my shoulder. "Grace, I didn't expect you to rescue me. I didn't expect anyone to. I didn't even know where the Hell I was. But I knew you would try, and that's enough. There's no way we could have seen this coming."

After her tears were dry, we continued our mission into town. There were people calmly walking down the streets, and businesses seemed to be open as they usually were. I took those things as good signs, but didn't stop to chat.

Standing outside the palace doors, I tried to think of any possible way we could get inside. I had a feeling that knocking wasn't going to do it for us. There was no other way in or out that I knew of, and if we wanted information, we needed it straight from the horse's mouth, so to speak.

"Maybe just one of us should knock and the other one hide. That way if we're captured, the other can get help," Grace suggested.

"Yes, because all of our plans always work out *exactly* like we think they will," I mumbled.

Grace looked at me like she was going to tear up again, and I realized I was punishing her for frustration she'd had no hand in causing.

"Sorry," I whispered.

"Well, do you have any other ideas?" she asked (not unkindly, which told me she'd accepted my apology).

About that time, the door opened, and Grace and I froze as we saw our own terror reflected back at us by the mirrored eyes of Hades. We had been found out, and now both of us were going to be locked away.

CHAPTER EIGHT

Fear ran through me like icy water; my knees tried to give way beneath me, and I wanted to cower in front of this man, this thing, this god.

Grace's hand found mine, and she squeezed it so hard that I whimpered, but the pain was good. It brought me back to myself, and I remembered she was there with me. I might not fight for myself as hard as I should, but I would protect her with every fiber of my being, even if she was the vampire and I was only human. I took a breath and pushed it all the way into my feet to steady myself, forcing myself to look past my own reflection in Hades's eyes.

"Why are you back?" His voice rolled across my skin, smoother than I remembered, and less menacing. "You must be a brave one." He looked Grace up and down. "And I see you brought a friend."

He didn't seem surprised that I had escaped, and he didn't strike me as angry—both points in my favor.

"We came to find out what's going on with all the freed souls. Persephone left me as reigning Queen, and when she comes back, I'll owe her an explanation." I hoped throwing his wife's name in there, and reminding him that she was coming back, might be useful.

I saw the faintest of smiles cross his lips—I amused him. "She won't be back for some time. All of the doors being open makes travel between the world of the living and dead a little more challenging than usual. As for telling you my plans, I think I'd rather let you find out on your own. I'll be making an announcement shortly." His eyes shined with a mischievous light.

"Let the poor girl in and tell her what you're doing. You owe her that much after locking her away in a tomb," Melinoe's voice called from behind the door.

Hades turned to glare at her. I couldn't see her face, but heard her say, "Besides, mum will be back at some point, and she's going to be pissed about how you treated her."

Relenting, Hades opened the door wide enough for us to come inside.

I leaned around the door without stepping in until I could see Melinoe. She was leaned back against a orange tree, peeling an orange with her black fingers.

She saw me, and the hesitation in my movements. "It's fine, come on inside. He won't harm you... again."

I stepped inside the palace, followed closely by Grace.

Hades still had on the black robe, and I had to fight not to think about what was under it. He brushed his hair back and ran his fingers through his dark beard. "And you are?" he asked Grace.

"Grace." She stood tall and held her hand out to him.

He waved her hand away. "Vampire," he growled,

and rolled his eyes, stepping closer to me.

That was the first moment since I'd been here that I almost wished I was a vampire. He was standing way too close, hovering just a breath away from touching me. I could smell him. He smelled like rich, fresh dirt, heavy with minerals from decomposing things; he smelled like the sweet roses and lilies you'd find on caskets in funeral homes; and underneath, he smelled like saltwater. The combination of scents coming from his skin and hair fit with the scary/beautiful theme he had going.

"So…" he tapped his finger to his lips, "you want to know what I'm up to, do you?"

Out of the corner of my eye, I saw Melinoe motion for Grace to come and stand beside her. Grace went to the other woman, and I was glad.

I looked back at Hades. "Yes."

"That nasty vampire, Rasputin, did quite the job of muddying things across the afterlives. My wife should have never let Thaddeus handle retrieval and bargaining. Gods don't want to deal with a go-between: it's insulting. Some souls came back, and some weren't allowed to leave, and then there was begging from other souls for a chance to try out another afterlife. Since the gods didn't want to play nice, I just opened up the doorways myself, and everyone can choose where they want to go and stay. At some point, I'll close the doors again, and that's where the souls will stay." His eyes flashed with amusement. "Sort of like musical chairs!"

Souls wandering in and out of other afterlives, with angry gods roaming about—this did not sound good at all.

"Aren't all these other god's upset with what you've done?" I asked.

He shrugged and smirked, the right side of his mouth raising just a bit. He knew he was handsome.

"They were, but I told them to think of it as a game. There is potential for loss of souls in their worlds, yes." He held up a finger. "But there is also potential for growth! If they don't go around throwing temper tantrums and trying to capture the souls they claim belong to them, they could schmooze even more souls into joining them. It's a fresh start for all!" Hades seemed so proud of himself and his grand idea.

"And *all* of the gods of the afterlives are going along with this?" I asked.

"No, not all of them. Some gods just have no sense of humor, so they just kept the souls that belonged to them, and sent ours back. They sealed their doors and won't play with us." He rolled his eyes and turned to walk away.

I still had questions, so I followed. "Who all is participating in this? I mean are there souls running around from the Christian heaven, or Muslim heaven? Is Valhalla open to anyone after this?"

Hades stopped, and sighed, "No, the big God keeps heaven sealed up so tightly a flea couldn't sneak in, and He isn't one to participate in our dealings. He has his own set of rules. No one in Jannah seemed interested either. Really, so far in the competition, it's been us, Loki, and Lucifer."

The room swirled with this new information. "You mean Hell is open? Souls from Hell are free, and Satan is looking to claim more? People are wandering into Hell, asking themselves, 'Hmm, would I like to spend eternity in here?'" I couldn't even begin to process this on a logical level of understanding.

"Don't be ridiculous," Hades spat. "Lucifer would never allow souls to just walk away from Hell—no one would stay! Besides, Hell is nearly impossible to get to unless he takes you himself. That's part of the appeal for him: convincing souls to follow him, and then once they are there, it's too late," he winked.

"And you're fine with this? Souls suffering for all eternity because you were playing some game!" I shouted.

"Hey!" he roared at me. "I told you this was a fair game. We aren't allowed to lie about what our afterlife is, if we are asked directly. We can only sway with our charming personalities and wit. No false promises. I'll be making a public announcement later to let everyone know they are free to go about their time as it was, or choose a new location at their will. I'll also be introducing Loki and Lucifer, so that everyone knows who they are dealing with."

Somehow I wasn't reassured by this. I bit my lip, and tried to think of what else I could ask that would be useful.

"I figured you would be all about this. From what I hear, you enjoy reuniting people with their former lovers and families. This is an opportunity to do that for a lot of souls." The tone of his voice tried to make it sound as appealing as possible.

"It seems like that's information you wouldn't usually share," I said.

"The rules are a bit relaxed right now," he grinned.

My mind of course went straight to Raphael. Maybe this was my chance to find him and be with him, or at the very least, find him and get closure.

"OK, I have to prepare for my speech. Time for you and your little friend to go." Hades shooed me away with his hand.

I still didn't like him, but he hadn't tried to hurt me this time, and he had told me what was going on. "Thank you, Hades," I said with true sincerity in my voice.

He stopped, and gave me a slight bow of his head. "You are welcome."

Hades left the garden where we had been chatting, and suddenly my head was flooded with all of the sounds I had been tuning out to focus on him: namely, the rushing of water into the little pond. Beyond that, laughter.

I turned to see Melinoe and Grace with huge smiles plastered across their faces, laughing loudly and staring into each other's eyes. *Uh-oh.*

"Hey there. Seems like the two of you are enjoying yourselves," I said as I approached.

Melinoe smiled and brushed her hair back with her long delicate fingers; then she rubbed her left arm, and traced gentle lines down her tattooed forearm as she looked at Grace. "Hel, I had no idea you had such a fabulous and fascinating friend." Melinoe's voice was a little heavier than the other times I had heard her speak—a little lower, and her accent more defined.

I wasn't sure what to say or how to act. It was very clear that Melinoe was attracted to Grace, and the way Grace was staring into Melinoe's dark eyes, I was pretty sure it was mutual. I looked at Grace hard enough to make her break eye contact with Melinoe. She looked at me a bit sheepishly.

"She is pretty great," I replied to Melinoe.

I took Grace by the arm. "Thank you for getting him to let us inside and making sure that he didn't lock us away." I gave a slight laugh.

"Of course," she said. "Will you be coming to the assembly later?"

Melinoe looked at Grace when she asked the question, but darted her eyes my direction as well, to let me know I was included.

"Yes, we'll be there," Grace smiled.

"Wonderful, I look forward to seeing you again," Melinoe smiled.

I looked at the two women standing in front of one another—Melinoe, with her androgynous, striking looks that would make any man or woman take pause. She was still dressed in black, tactical-looking clothes, with weapons and tools peeking out of her outfit here and there. And Grace, with her sleek black hair, and her little pops of red against all of the black she wore—it was clear to see their styles complimented one another, and why their attraction would be so strong. I had nothing against Melinoe, but I found myself suddenly defensive of Boude

"Yes, we best be getting back," I said to Grace. "I'm sure Boude is worried about you."

Grace glared at me for half of a second, and then I saw guilt cross her face. She turned back to Melinoe, a little less flirty than before. "Yes, it's been nice meeting you. See you later."

CHAPTER NINE

"What was that about?" I asked Grace as we headed back into the streets.

"What?" she asked, like she had no idea what I was talking about.

"Grace, there was some serious sexual tension between you and Melinoe," I said.

"Yeah, I thought she seemed a bit flirty," Grace mused.

"It wasn't just her. You were putting off the vibes too... which would be fine, if you didn't have a boyfriend."

Grace made a sound like she was going to protest, but stopped herself when she knew she didn't have an argument. She twisted a piece of hair around her finger and chewed on her lip. "She's really pretty, isn't she?"

"Yes, she's gorgeous—and that accent!" I cooed.

"Oh my God, I know right!" she gushed.

"Boude," I said to her.

Grace rubbed her head like she had a headache. "Yeah, Boude."

I didn't add anything else to the conversation,

even though I could have drawn it out with different scenarios, and tried to offer more words of wisdom. This was just something else she needed to figure out on her own.

We stopped in one of the small shops on our way back to the Quarter to pick up some snacks and drinks for everyone. All of the people in the store were buzzing about the big announcement being made later at the Assignment Hall.

I found myself wondering how many of them were supposed to be here, and how many of them were just checking things out from other worlds. It was impossible to tell, now that the drifting, ethereal spirits from other realms had solidified.

Grace and I hurried through the store, getting liquor and snacks that didn't require a refrigerator, since the vampire's mansion didn't have a kitchen.

A thought occurred to me. "Grace, when is the last time you and Boude went above to feed? Were things different?"

She stopped and thought for a moment. "We just pop in and out, but it's been a few days. I haven't noticed anything strange."

"I was just curious, since Hades had said going back and forth was difficult right now."

"I think it might be easier for us, because we don't have souls," she shrugged.

I thought about her statement. "If we could find Thaddeus and get him to tell us where we could find Persephone, you and Boude might be the only ones who could travel there and find her."

"We would be happy to, but where would we find Thaddeus?" Grace asked.

"I have no idea," I confessed. I remembered the bar that he used to frequent, but had a feeling that during all of this commotion, he was keeping himself out the way.

After bagging up our things, we headed back out into the streets and back into the Quarter. I figured we had just enough time to get everyone together and get back to the Assignment Hall before Hades made his big announcement.

"Why do we need to go if you just told us what he's going to say?" Andreas asked, still laying across the chaise in nearly the same position we had left him in.

"Because, shouldn't we know what Loki and Lucifer look like in case we run into them?" I asked.

"Yes, I would very much like to know what they look like," he grinned.

"Andreas, you cannot try to seduce one, or both of them," I said, already feeling tired.

"But why not? It's a perfect opportunity." He was genuinely appalled at the idea of doing anything else.

I looked around the room at the faces of our friends. Everyone was trying to cover their amusement, and no one was willing to help me explain why seducing the God of Mischief and the King of Darkness was a bad idea.

I shook my head in defeat. "Go for it," I said.

Andreas smiled and sat up, shaking out his golden hair a little where it had flattened from his earlier position. "I'll be upstairs getting dressed," he said, as he stood and took off up the stairs.

"Well, at least he's motivated now," said Ray with a chuckle.

The rest of us quickly followed suit. I cleaned myself up a little more, and wished that I'd had more clothes to change into.

Reading my mind, Grace popped her head into my room. "I know we're not exactly the same size, but I'm sure I have something you can wear if you want to change," she said.

"That would be great!" I said, and followed her into the room where her clothes were laid out on the bed, and Boude was looking in the mirror as he adjusted his vest. He wore a black shirt, and black vest with a faint embroidered pattern; the vest was double breasted, and set off by the rows of silver buttons. Normally he wore greens and golds to accent his emerald eyes and red hair. This was a different look on him; he looked intense, and almost threatening. But, I had to say, he still looked damn good.

Grace passed by him without much more than a blink, and started handing me things she thought would fit. She had more curves than I, but a lot of her clothes were stretchy, so they could work for either of us; they would just look very different, depending on which body they were adorning.

I picked up a pair of black leggings that had bands of leather running across them in different areas. I unbuttoned my jeans to try them on, but hesitated when I remembered Boude was in the room; he was so quiet I had almost forgotten. My hesitation was apparently very obvious because they both laughed.

"I promise to avert my eyes if you want to change in here," said Boude, as he eyed me in the mirror's reflection.

"Who cares," said Grace, "he's seen it all before anyway."

Boude actually blushed and looked away. "Something we were all trying to avoid saying, my love."

I was red now too; I could feel it creeping up my face. Having slept with your best friend's boyfriend was just something that didn't need to be brought up, no matter how long ago the situation had been.

"Yes, well tact is not Grace's strong suit." I cast a scolding look her way.

She shrugged. "Not a big deal. Try on the pants."

I did try on the pants, and was surprised at how well they fit me. I paired them with a deep purple top that fit me nicely, even through the chest—something that rarely happened, since I'm made smaller than most women.

"How do you keep your boobs in this shirt?" I asked Grace, who was considerably larger than I in that department.

Boude let out a startled laugh at my bluntness.

"I have particular bra I wear with shirts like that—keeps them in check," she winked.

I nodded.

"You look good," Grace complimented, and Boude agreed.

"Guess I'm ready," I said as I laced up my black work boots. Grace and I did not wear the same size shoe, and I would probably fall and kill myself in most of her getups. So my boots would have to do. They actually didn't look half bad.

A crowd had already gathered by the time we reached the Assignment Hall. I tried to keep my eyes open for Thaddeus, and a small part of me always looked for Raphael wherever I went.

We excused ourselves as far as people would allow, until we were almost at the front of the building.

Melinoe was already standing on one side of the door, and at her back were two ghosts so transparent you barely noticed them. She saw us and waved, but directed her wink only at Grace. Oh how I wished this was the only situation I needed to be worried about right now.

Grace beamed back at her and gave a small wave. Boude leaned in to ask who she was waving at, and gave a nod of satisfaction when Grace explained. I was fairly certain she had left out a few bits of information.

Silence rolled through the crowd like a wave as the door to the Hall opened, and out stepped Hades. I had yet to see him in anything besides the black robe, and found it a bit cliché at this point. I mean, yes, you're the God of the Underworld, but you don't have to look the part all of the time. I don't carry my shovel when I'm strolling around town.

However, looking beyond the robe, it was easy to tell you were looking at powerful being. The energy rolled off of him. It didn't feel bad, but it had a heaviness to it—a somberness. When he was around, you would be still and listen.

I recalled meeting Persephone, and the power that rolled off of her: how I had liked her instantly—loved her, even. I wondered what it would feel like to be in the same room with the couple.

Hades's voice was powerful as he spoke of all of these "new opportunities for free choice" now being offered in the underworld.

As he spoke, I watched many emotions play across the faces of the people around us. Some people were excited about getting to shorten their sentences, or changing their soul's destination. Others were nervous about new souls moving in without having first followed the rules and being assigned. Some people were disappointed that all the different gods weren't participating, which I understood. *I mean, if you get to pick, shouldn't you get to learn about all of them?* I thought. And others were relieved we didn't have to worry about *all* the gods running around our part of the underworld—which I also understood. There were a few old gods I didn't want to meet.

The time came where Hades was ready to introduce the crowd to the other participants in his little game.

Loki was the first one that Hades called forth. Loki wasn't quite what I was expecting. He was tall and slim, with reddish blonde hair, cut short and neatly. His face was clean shaven, and held a boyish charm that was endearing—and untrustworthy. I could hear him telling a neighborhood lady all about how *he* hadn't been the one to break her window with the baseball, but he saw the boy who did—all while having his fingers crossed behind his back.

It was the kind of face you knew better than to trust, but really wanted to try. I had known a lot of people like that, and I saw right through them. I didn't like him.

Loki's voice sounded like a sweet young baptist preacher, full of hope, and inspiration about how to serve God and your fellow man—all while he banged the pretty sunday school teachers, and stole from the offering plate… and people were eating it up. Everyone wanted to go see Valhalla and Folkvangr after his speech was over. I doubted Odin approved of what was happening here.

   Next up was the one I dreaded. I hadn't even believed in the devil when I died; I never could have dreamed I would be waiting to hear him make a speech to try to convince people to follow him to Hell. I felt nauseated just waiting for him to step out of the shadows, and then questioned myself on if he could really be as bad as I had heard, or if it was just so much conditioning causing this response.

   He did step out of the shadows, and he gave his spiel about the perks of choosing his path. But I don't know what he said, or what the reactions were of the people around me. I stood in stunned silence as I watched Lucifer speak—only I had known him as my Raphael.

CHAPTER TEN

My Raphael: his long black hair was straight and shining as it laid over his shoulders and hung down his back. His pants were black, and he wore a blue t-shirt underneath a tailored black jacket: casual, yet stylish. His blue eyes sparkled even from a distance, and I thought of those same eyes watching me from my bed, as I moved across the room to him the night we first made love. More intimate flashes flooded my mind, and the whole world swayed. *Dear God, I had sex with the devil?*

Everything became even fuzzier as he finished his speech, and when I came to, I could hear voices before my vision cleared.

"No way, is that what you think happened to her?" one male voice said.

"I'm telling you, it looked just like him. That must've been what spooked her," the other man said.

"Hel, Hel! Are you awake? Are you hurt?" My senses were clearing up, and I knew the voice speaking to me now was Grace.

"Tell me I imagined all of that." My eyes pleaded with those of everyone around me.

"What do you think you imagined?" Boude asked.

"Raphael…" I swallowed and tasted bile. "He was Lucifer," I choked out.

"We've never seen him, love. No idea if that was him—maybe just a lookalike," Ray said.

I shook my head no. "Billy, you saw him when I dug him up. Wasn't that him?"

Billy shook his head, and stammered, "Aw, Hel, I don't know. I mean sure, it looked like him, but I've never talked to the guy, and when you dug him up, we were more focused on you."

Andreas was standing to the side with an annoyed look on his face.

"What is it?" I asked him.

"I hope it wasn't him. It will be very anticlimactic for me to sleep with the devil if you've already beat me to it," he said, and he was serious.

I stood up faster than I should have, and everything started to spin again. Even so, I lunged for Andreas, and a sound came out of my throat that I'd never heard before. I was not in the mood for his shit.

Billy and Grace pulled me back, while Andreas had the nerve to look shocked. Boude grabbed Andreas by the arm and quickly led him away from me.

"I need to talk to him," I said, and I leaned my head against Billy's shoulder until I could raise it without puking or passing out again.

"I'm sure Boude will bring him back after you've calmed down," he tried to comfort me.

"Not Andreas! Raphael, Lucifer… whoever the fuck that was," I groaned. "Did any of you see where he went?"

"We were all a little focused on you fainting,"

Margaret said as she stroked my hair.

I couldn't lose him until I had the chance to talk to him and find out what was happening. "Grace, go to Melinoe and ask where I can find Lucifer, or if she can set up a meeting."

Grace looked shocked that I had asked her to go to Melinoe, but smiled and ran off immediately to do just that. I knew it was a terribly selfish request to ask Grace to put herself in that position to help me, but I'd feel guilty about it later.

I was still leaning on Billy, but slowly putting more of my weight on my own feet and trusting them to hold me up. Billy was more of a safety blanket now, rather than the total support system he was a few moments ago.

"Hel, are you OK?"

I knew the voice, and forced myself to be as hard as stone before I faced him. I turned and looked at Soren. Eira wasn't by his side for a change. "I am. Thanks for checking. How are you?" I asked.

He looked at little shaken, and ran his fingers through his beard. "I'm fine. Was that who I think it was?" he asked, pointing towards the area where the speakers had been.

I was surprised he had remembered Raphael's face so well after only seeing it briefly. But now that I had seen Eira's, I wasn't likely to forget it either.

I nodded. "I think so. I'm trying to set up a meeting to find out," I said.

Soren took my hand in his, and it caught me so off guard that I pulled it back quickly. Soren looked like I had just slapped him in the face. His eyes fell downward, and wouldn't meet mine any longer.

"Please be careful, Hel," he said, and walked away.

Dammit, why now! my mind screamed. I didn't want to hurt Soren. I didn't want him to be miserable with Eira. I didn't want the love of my life to be Satan. I laid my head back down on Billy's shoulder, and Ray took my hand in his. I didn't pull away from him.

The crowd was thinning as everyone made their way into their separate corners of the underworld, either to work or explore. I just wanted Grace to hurry back so I could know what to do next.

I would have waited in that spot as long as it took, but after a while without Grace or Boude's return, my remaining friends encouraged me to head back to the mansion and rest. The vampires knew where to find us.

To my surprise, when we walked in the door Boude was waiting on the couch. He stood, and stretched when he saw us. "Don't worry, Andreas isn't here; he said he was going to look for Loki. I figured that was better than being in your way."

I just stared at him and tried to think of what to say. I gave up quickly, since my mouth didn't seem to work anymore. I hoped talking was a skill I would recall when the time came to talk to Raphael, or whoever he might be.

"Do you want to be with everyone, or do you want to go to your room and be alone?" Margaret asked. She had been stroking my hair and shoulders soothingly, and watching out for my every step on the way back from the city. It was my guess she had been a mom in life—probably a really good one, too.

"In here's fine," I whispered. I really didn't want to be alone, I just didn't have the energy required to do anything more than sitting and staring at my feet.

Margaret held my hand and walked me to the couch, where I promptly sat down like my ass had weights in it.

"Do you want a blanket, tea, anything at all?"

I nodded, "Both." I could feel myself shivering, but I knew the temperature of the room was fine—it was just the shock, and honestly, the blanket probably wouldn't help that.

Boude wrapped the blanket around my shoulders, and soon, Margaret brought me a cup of tea.

"Where is our Grace?" Boude asked.

"Hel sent her to find Raphael and set up a meeting or something," Billy told him.

Worry passed Boude's face, but he said nothing about it. "I'm sure she will be returning soon."

I certainly hoped so.

My friends stopped waiting for me to talk finally, and started talking between themselves—asking one another if they were staying here with the way things were, or going to explore other avenues. Ray thought it would be fascinating to explore Valhalla, while Billy and Margaret planned to stay and work off their time in hopes of getting into heaven at some point. Boude didn't care either way, since he was a vampire, but said he found it "fascinating how religion drives the every motive of mortals."

The front door swung open and Grace walked in, all smiles, looking incredibly proud of herself.

I was on my feet the second I saw her. "Did you find

out where he is? Can I meet him?" I grilled her before she could even close the door.

"Even better," she glowed, and behind her, in stepped Raphael.

I threw the blanket aside and ran to him. I planned to jump into his arms, and kiss him with every ounce of the desire that had been building up inside of me since I had left him. My eyes were locked on his as I came towards him, but I stopped just short of throwing myself at him. One thing was clear: he wasn't as excited to see me as I was him.

I still took his hands in mine. "Don't you recognize me?" I asked.

"Helena?" he asked.

"Yes!" I cheered hopefully.

"Grace told me that's your name, and that you believe you know me—that I was to come and see you so that we could catch up." He left his hands in mine, but stepped back from me just a fraction of an inch.

My heart fell a little at his aversion. It was clear he didn't recognize me.

"Raphael, don't you remember when we were alive and you met me in the cemetery? You helped me dig a grave, and then we were going to travel together." I tried to fit our entire short story into a few words and breaths.

He looked at me solemnly and shook his head. "I'm very sorry, my dear. You must have me confused with someone else. I am Lucifer, not this Raphael you speak of. I have never walked on the earth as a mortal; though this love story of yours sounds quite intriguing, it is not me you search for."

This time he did take his hands out of mine and

stepped a full step back. "I must be getting back to town. This trial only lasts so long, and I have campaigning to do, so to speak." He smiled, and gave a friendly wave to everyone in the room.

I stared at him blankly; he looked and sounded exactly like my Raphael. How could he not know—how could he break my heart again like this and just leave me?

As he walked towards the door, he stopped to admire his reflection in the large gold mirror that hung in the entryway. He smoothed a piece of hair back over his shoulder, then snapped his fingers as he turned to me.

"Of course!" he said. "It's my host. I don't like for people to see my true form—it gives the wrong impression—so I borrow shells from some of my souls to use when I'm away from home. This must belong to the man you speak of." Lucifer looked down at the body he was inhabiting. "Mystery solved!"

CHAPTER ELEVEN

HE WAS HALFWAY OUT THE DOOR WHEN I REACHED out and grabbed him by the back of his jacket. I was tempted to grab him by his hair, but didn't want to risk hurting Raphael if this was actually his body.

"Wait!" I yelled. "You can't just leave after telling me that!"

Lucifer turned back to me with a smile, and now I could see more clearly than before that this most certainly was not my Raphael, no matter how much he looked like him.

"Take your hands off of me, little girl." The words trickled out from between his smiling lips, and I shivered so hard I thought my skin was trying to crawl off.

"Just tell me how to get to him, the one you took the shell from. How do I get him back?" I begged.

"You don't get people back from Hell," he scoffed.

"But the rules don't apply right now! You're free to recruit as many souls as you can to take back to Hell. You won't miss just this one."

"I assure you that I would," he said.

"Please!" I begged again.

"You are welcome to come and join him," said Lucifer. "That's my final offer."

"I wi…" is all I managed to say, before a hand was firmly clamped over my mouth and I couldn't finish my sentence.

"Hel, I'm not letting you make this decision this impulsively. There's always another way," Ray whispered in my ear.

I struggled against him for a moment, and then stopped and breathed.

"So this is where the action is happening!" a new voice called from behind Lucifer in the doorway.

All of us were surprised to see Loki standing there, still all in white.

"Um, hello," Boude said, and even the classiest vampire sounded surprised. He gave the god one of his more graceful bows. "It's an honor to have you here. Is there a reason you are calling on us?"

About that time, Andreas stepped in, looking flawless as usual, dressed in a red shirt that clung to his golden skin, and tan suede pants that hugged everything just right. His hair looked like spun gold, and his amber eyes reflected every hint of light in the room. I hated that he was so pretty; I couldn't help but stare, even when I was upset with him.

Andreas came up beside Loki and put his hand on his shoulder. "He is my guest," Andreas smiled.

Of course…

"I am, but I had no idea so many fascinating things would be going on here!" he teased. "I do hope you'll forgive me, but I was eavesdropping a bit before we came in." Loki smiled that boyish grin that made me nervous. "I might be able to help." He looked at

Lucifer. "May I propose an idea?"

Lucifer, who was now looking less and less like Raphael to me, arched an eyebrow at the other man. Between Lucifer being dressed nearly all in black, and Loki being all in white, it almost looked like a battle of good and evil. But I knew the stories about Loki, and I knew that was far from what this was.

"You may propose your idea, but that doesn't mean that I will accept it," Lucifer said plainly.

"Fair enough," said Loki before continuing. "What if she can find her way to Hell, and retrieve this Raphael's soul without your assistance? Let her journey to Hell, and get back. If she makes it, she and her boyfriend get to stay." Loki smiled like he was super proud of this plan. I, on the other hand, was suddenly both excited, and scared out of my mind.

Lucifer laughed, "There's no way she could make it!"

"Then what do you have to lose? If she doesn't, then you have an extra soul that you didn't have win over," Loki shrugged.

I honestly wasn't sure if he was trying to help me, or just wanted to watch and see what happened.

"She would have to find the entrance herself," Lucifer said, seeming to think over the idea.

Loki nodded in agreement, and added, "And of course, no other person could go with her."

"No, no other people could accompany her," he agreed, and then snapped his head around to look at Grace and Boude. "And no vampires," he added.

"Naturally," said Loki.

Lucifer looked at me. "You have to be back with his soul by the time the doors close."

"But we don't know when that will be," I said.

He shrugged, "Well then you better travel fast." He walked to the doorway to depart. "Leave as soon as you're ready, and watch out for demons."

"You're welcome!" Loki smiled like he'd just taken out the trash for me, and cheerfully followed Andreas (who was the most single minded person/vampire that I had ever met) up the stairs and off to his room.

My name was coming at me from all directions. "Hel, you can't! You wouldn't! It's too risky," were all things being lectured in my direction.

Meanwhile, my mind was full of questions: *Why is Raphael in Hell? What does one pack to take to Hell? Where is the entrance? How far is it? Who can answer these damn questions for me?* I had an answer to my last question, at least.

I sighed, and left my friends staring at me as I said, "I have to go see Hades," and ran out the still-open door.

"You never go away, do you?" Hades chuckled, as I barged into the palace and into the living room, where he was talking with Melinoe. The huge three-headed dog sat by his side, panting and drooling on the floor. I wondered how Persephone would have felt about that, it being her place and all.

"I need to speak with you. It's urgent."

He actually looked surprised, and motioned for me to sit down beside him. "Melinoe, would you excuse us for a bit?" Hades looked to Melinoe, who had her own look of surprise on her face.

I held up my hand. "That isn't necessary; she can hear what I have to say, and might be able to help as well."

Melinoe remained seated, and now they both were watching me with intrigue.

I told them about my reaction to seeing Lucifer at the assembly, and about Grace bringing him to me at the mansion. Melinoe nodded up until that part of the story, since she had been the one to aid Grace in finding him for me. I went on to tell them about Loki and the arrangements that were made.

"My my, you have had a busy time." Hades raised his eyebrows and sipped something out of a nearby goblet.

Cerberus whined at my feet, and I instinctively reached my hand down to pet the giant pup.

"I wouldn't—" Hades started to say, but quieted as the dog wagged it's long tail, and all three heads covered my arm with kisses. He shook his head in amazement.

"He won't even let me do that!" Melinoe commented in her down-under accent.

I shrugged. "Animals have always liked me."

"So what is it you think I can do for you?" Hades returned to the conversation I had started.

"I need you to tell me where the entrance to Hell is, and how I can get in, get Raphael, and get out—and I need you to promise me you won't close the doors until I'm back." I didn't know whether I should be demanding or pleading, so I made my voice firm, but kept my eyes soft.

"Why would I help you do these things—isn't that cheating?" he asked.

"You do kind of owe her," Melinoe remarked.

"For throwing her in the tomb? I admitted that was a bit impulsive. How many favors could I possibly owe her for that?" He held his hands up like we were overreacting.

I said, "I don't actually remember you admitting that, but if you do this for me, I swear I'll call it even forever."

He seemed to think this over. "You won't tell Persephone when she gets back?"

I shook my head. "Not a word." Of course, I had wanted to tell her, but this was much more important, and I could live without watching the queen avenge me—fun as it might be.

"Very well. Even with all of the help I can give you, there's a very good chance you won't make it back. Lucifer has demons stationed everywhere, and they don't mess around."

"I understand," I said. Internally I was asking myself why the Hell I was doing this. *Shouldn't I be worried about my own soul? Shouldn't I just work off my time and go to heaven, or wherever?* The word "love" echoed through my head like the vibration from a bass drum. Love was almost always the answer to any question asking why people did stupid things. "What should I take with me?" I asked.

Hades smirked. "You'll need a shovel."

CHAPTER TWELVE

Hades sent Melinoe with me to collect the shovel, and few things I thought I might need. Walking back into the fields of the dead made me homesick.

"Are you sure you want to go to Hell?" Melinoe asked.

"No, but I'm sure I have to try to save Raphael, if I can." I walked through the brown dirt quickly, glancing down now and then, hoping to see a name of someone waiting to be unearthed.

"Have you thought about why he might be in Hell? Maybe that's where he belongs…"

That hadn't occurred to me; I wasn't capable of believing that Raphael could have ever done anything so bad that he would be damned. It had to be a mistake—it *had* to be.

I walked by Soren's house, and all was quiet. All of the other reapers were gone, and all the little houses were empty, except for his, which only made it all feel stranger.

I was tempted to knock on the door and just say hello, but I didn't want to start trouble or upset Eira, so I walked on by.

The doors on the shed squeaked and moaned as I opened them. We didn't have assigned shovels or flashlights, but we all had our favorites. The one I had chosen was just right for my height, and had a sharper edge than the others. The dirt moved away easily here in the underworld, unlike in the living world, where you sometimes had to break the hardened dirt apart before you could shovel it away. But I still liked the shovel that I knew I would have preferred back at home in the cemetery. You couldn't really tell the flashlights apart to choose a favorite, so I just grabbed one.

Melinoe was leaned back against the shed, flicking one of the lights on and off while she waited for me. Her ghostly bodyguards were quiet today, and stayed well back from us. They had been easy to ignore.

She had loaned me a black backpack with lots of straps and hidden compartments. I was trying to decide where to put the flashlight in case I needed easy access to it, and how the Hell I was going to carry this shovel with me on my journey—a journey I still didn't know the length or difficulty of.

A huge hand was suddenly on the shed door above my head.

"What are you doing here?" Soren asked me. I couldn't say that I was surprised he had heard me out here, with all the racket I was making.

"I have to go somewhere, and needed some supplies," I told him. I tried to keep my face as neutral as I could.

"Where?" The one question felt more like he had asked one thousand.

"Hell," I said simply.

Soren's gray eyes widened, and anger washed across his face.

I pointed a finger at him. "No. You don't get to look at me like that. You know as well as I do that we would do whatever it takes to save someone that we love. You would have left me in a split second to save Eira, if you had had a way to get her back and knew she was in Hell."

He looked away from me then. "I *would* have."

I closed my eyes and tried to find my breath. I knew Soren well enough to know what he was saying in those few words. *He would have before, but wouldn't now.*

"Where is she?" I asked him, not being able to hold onto my anger.

"In the house. She never leaves," he sighed.

I hated seeing him this way: defeated. I knew I needed to go. I had things to do, and Billy was right: Soren was a big boy. He needed to handle his own shit. I couldn't just leave, though. I did love Soren.

"What happened with her, Soren? Is *this* the woman you grieved over for centuries?" I couldn't help the disdain in my voice.

He looked embarrassed. "I don't remember. I held onto that idea of what love was for so long, I don't remember what our marriage was really like, or if it was fantasies I imagined to be real."

I put my hand on his shoulder. "What does she say? Does she still love you?"

"She says that she does, but she remembers things differently from our life together. She says I tried to control her, and was mean at times, but I don't remember. I waited for her after I died, but she went on to her next life without even looking for me. She says she became a successful woman in her last lifetime, and that the husband she had was better to her than I was. I'm trying to make up for the things I did, I just don't remember." A tear rolled down his cheek and he quickly brushed it away. "I am a terrible man. I was a bad husband, and now that I have the opportunity to make things better, I'm even worse, because my mind keeps turning back to you." He met my eyes once more.

Oh my God, I cannot deal with this right now! I rubbed my eyes and tried to think of what to say.

"Soren, you are NOT a bad man, I have never seen an ounce of unjustified anger in you. I have never seen you lash out. Eira was so high on the pedestal you put her on that no one ever could have been that special, even her. I have a hard time believing the things she says about you while the two of you were married, but she has to let that go. Neither of you are the same people anymore. I think she's manipulating you—to what end, I don't know. You are stronger than that. If she keeps talking about her last husband, let her go find him. You found her; you're trying. If that's not enough, it's time to end this and let your soul go wherever it feels led."

"So you don't think of me—of us—anymore?" he asked.

I sighed, and every ounce of imaginary air left my body, down to my toes. "I try really hard not to."

"You don't want me, even if she left and your Raphael didn't return?"

"Soren, don't do this to me," I begged.

He nodded, and turned to walk away. I stopped him by grabbing his hand and giving it a squeeze. He turned back to me with a deep longing in his eyes.

I closed the distance between us and kissed him. He kissed me back with the ferocity that I remembered and loved so much. I wanted more of him, all of him, the way I had had him so many times: with tongues, and teeth, and scratching and screaming, until we were sticky with sweat and too tired to move. But after a moment, I broke the kiss and pulled away from his tight embrace.

"You settle things with Eira, whatever needs to be done. I'm going to get Raphael. If I come back, we will see where we stand," I said. My voice was distant as I pushed the emotions away so that I could function.

Soren cupped the side of my face in his palm. The gesture made me feel small and delicate. "I don't care if you come back with him. Just come back, Helena."

I nodded as I stared into those cold-steel eyes, and this time when he walked away, I didn't stop him.

"Wow, that was intense as fuck," said Melinoe as she stepped around the side of the shed door.

I jumped, having nearly forgotten she was there. "Did you just stand there and watch all of that happen?"

"Well it all happened kind of fast, and neither of you seemed to care that I was there. I was afraid it would have been more disruptive to call attention myself by moving."

I really couldn't argue with her on that.

"OK," I said, "how do I get to Hell?"

I was back in the dungeon where I had been entombed.

I cringed as I walked by the stone coffin and saw that the lid was closed.

"Don't worry, no one is in it right now," said Hades, noticing my lingering stare.

That only made me feel slightly better.

Hades was leading the way with Cerberus by his side, and Melinoe was at his back with her two guards on either side. I brought up the back, but would have preferred being in the middle. I didn't like feeling like someone could sneak up on me.

I gasped suddenly as a realization hit me. *I didn't say goodbye to anyone!* I'd left the mansion in such a hurry, and I had never gone back to tell them anything that I learned or decided. Guilt overwhelmed me, and I almost stopped walking—almost said that I had to turn around and go to my friends. But I knew if I left, there was a very big chance that Hades wouldn't be as generous next time—and I also wouldn't have put it past my friends to lock me up and not let me leave. I wouldn't even blame them. I would have done the same to them. It did make me sad, though, that it hadn't hit my mind until just now. I had people who loved me and wanted me safe. For most of my life it just been Ray that cared for me, and once he was gone, I was on my own for a long time. I felt so bad doing this to them, but I knew it was much too late to turn back.

"Melinoe," I called to her.

She slowed her pace to walk alongside me. "Yes?"

"Can you look in on my friends for me, please? I didn't tell them that I was leaving so soon. They'll be worried sick, and angry with me. Tell them I'm sorry, and that I love them, and I'll do my best to get back to them." *I won't cry.*

"Yes, I will tell them," she said as she walked along.

I caught her forearm and made her look at me. "Promise me." I was closer to her face than I had been before, and I was still struck at how she managed to be both handsome and beautiful at the same time.

"I promise," she said keeping full eye contact.

We resumed walking down the long tunnels, and I couldn't help but feel like I was walking towards the death chamber in a prison—which was mildly amusing, since I was already dead, but there were many different ways a person could die.

"Tell me about Grace," Melinoe said.

"Why?" I asked, as if I didn't have an inkling.

"She seems fascinating. I've never spent much time around any vampires, and her scars are marvelous." Melinoe sounded almost breathless as she said the last part.

"Grace is very young," I said first. "She hasn't been turned long. She was a suicide that I reaped. I signed for her because she was underage, and we became best friends. She works at the boutique Andreas runs in town. He was her maker," I said.

"And who is the dapper red-headed vamp that's around her?" Melinoe asked.

"That's Boude, her boyfriend." I looked at her while I said it.

"Are they serious?"

I wanted to tell her that they were, and she needed to back off and not ruin my best friend's relationship, but that wasn't my place. "I believe that he is serious about her."

"She doesn't return his level of feelings?" Melinoe

pressed.

"Like I said, Grace is very young," I said once more.

I saw a slight smile cross Melinoe's lips as she realized she might stand a shot at Grace. I liked Melinoe, but I also liked Boude. Boude had proven himself more of a relationship person than I had imagined, and I knew he loved Grace. Melinoe was sexy, and striking, but she seemed like someone who would just want to have fun. Maybe Grace wanted to explore other people, since Boude was the only healthy relationship she'd ever been in. Maybe she just wanted to have fun and not be so serious for a while. Again, it wasn't my call to make. I just hoped that I made it back from this to see what she decided.

I was suddenly feeling claustrophobic. The ceilings were getting lower, and the tunnel was becoming narrow. My heart was beating hard, and I had to keep reminding myself the thudding wasn't real.

"Almost there," Hades announced from in front of us.

We were all having to walk single file now, even the big black dog, who's claws clicked against the stone floor.

The gas lanterns on the wall were fewer and farther between, giving the already creepy space an even eerier glow from the flickering flames. *Flames. Hell, what was I thinking?*

CHAPTER THIRTEEN

We stopped where the tunnel ended. It was a wide spot, just large enough for us to stand together.

I looked at the walls and floor, everything was stone. "Are we in the right place?" I asked. "Did we miss a door?"

"This is it," Hades said, and the way he shifted from foot to foot, and kept eyeing the tunnel back to the main areas made me uncomfortable.

"Well, what now?" I asked.

Melinoe looked to her step-father for clues; she didn't know any more than I did.

Hades took a cold torch down from the wall and lit it from the flame of one of the gas lanterns. "Step back," he said.

We all backed up until our backs hit the wall, which was only a step or two. Hades leaned down with the torch in hand, and seemed to be looking for something on the floor. "Ah," he said after a moment. He touched the fire to the floor, and flames shot up in a rush of heat and power, like a geyser made of fire.

Melinoe and I covered our faces from the heat, and Cerberus whined and moved closer to me. Unable to avoid the flames, Hades patted out the small fires that were burning on his robe. His skin and hair were untouched, and he only looked mildly annoyed.

The fire slowly shrank, from being so tall it was over our heads, to the size of a small campfire. As it burned, an odor filled the tunnel; it was so pungent that even Hades covered his face.

"What is that?" Melinoe asked, pinching her nose and coughing.

"It smells like sulfur," I said.

The fire slowly faded out, and where the stone floor had just been was a perfect circle of a pale yellow substance. Hades swiped his finger through the powder and recoiled at the scent.

"Otherwise known as brimstone," he said. He dusted his hands off and began walking back towards the tunnel. "We'll leave you to it."

"What do I do now?" I asked, still as confused as ever.

"Honestly, I led you here, and even opened the door. Must I spell it all out for you?" He turned to the circle filled with the vile smelling powder and pointed. "Under there—start digging."

"Good luck," Melinoe said, as she turned to leave me too.

I took a shaky breath and sank my shovel into the circle as far as it would go. I removed scoop after scoop of brimstone from the hole, and it never seemed to make a dent, even though the pile beside me was starting to grow.

The longer I dug, the more frustrated I became. "Dammit," I yelled at no one, and dropped my shovel in frustration.

I hear a whimper, and then felt something nuzzle my waist. I looked down to see one of Cerberus's heads against me, while the other two panted.

"Hey boy... boys," I said, and scratched each head behind the ears. The dog's tail wagged like mad, and then slowed as my disappointment resumed.

Cerberus, like all dogs, could tell I was unhappy. He looked at the spot where I had been digging, and back to me.

"There's too much. I don't think I can get through it all," I told him, because it wasn't like talking to a three-headed dog was the strangest thing I'd done lately.

The dog snorted, ran to the hole, and began digging furiously; brimstone was flying out of the hole and all over the tunnel.

"What a good boy!" I praised him as I watched him do his best to help me.

He worked tirelessly, as fast as he could go, but when all three mouths were hanging open and panting, I stopped him. We were both yellow with the powder, and the poor dog had yellow tongues—I knew that couldn't taste good. I wished that I had water to give him.

Looking down, it appeared that we had maybe made the tiniest dent in the brimstone-filled hole.

"Fuck," I sighed. The dog joined me in swearing by letting out a very annoyed whine.

I looked around for other ideas, and my eyes fell back on the torch. Digging wasn't going to do it this time, and the brimstone had to be out of the way for me to get through. I hoped that by lighting only the brimstone in the hole, the fire would be contained, and not spread through the tunnel, or over me and the dog.

Just to be on the safe side, I dusted us off the best I could, and made Cerberus stand as far away as I could get him. I tossed the lit torch into the center of the brimstone circle, expecting the same reaction as last time. But flames didn't shoot up, and the tunnel didn't fill with fire. Instead, it looked as though the fire was melting the brimstone.

The abundant yellow powder started to glow red as the fire sank down into it. The hole became deeper and deeper, until all of the red and yellow was gone, and there was emptiness. I smiled at the effectiveness of my ingenuity, and then realized I was going to have to go into that hole, and the smile vanished.

I sat on the edge of the stone floor and dangled my feet down into the hole, trying to work up the nerve to jump in. *Well, this is the last thing I ever wanted to do,* I thought.

Cerberus was by my side, sniffing the opening and backing away.

"Don't worry, bud. There's no way I'm letting you come with me," I told him. "I'd never forgive myself if something happened to you."

The head on the left barked at me as if to say, "But I'm supposed to protect YOU!"

I shook my head at him. "Go back to your master."

The head on the left snorted again, and I wondered if each head had its own personality.

"Well, if you want to stay, that's fine. But stay here. I might need you to help pull me out when I get back."

He laid down and rested his heads on the floor facing the hole.

"Guess I need to get this started," I told myself. And before I could second guess myself for another moment, I jumped.

The scene from Alice in Wonderland played in my mind: the one of her falling and falling down the rabbit hole. The image in my mind was all I saw, though, and I hit something before my brain could translate the image to the thought of, *I wonder how long I'll fall.*

The landing wasn't what I would have called easy, but I didn't hurt, so that was good. The bad part was that I was in total darkness and didn't know if I should turn left or right, forward or back. Panic started to overwhelm me, and I couldn't move. *Oh God, what if I'm stuck here in the darkness forever?* It was just too awful a thing to think about. Even though I didn't need to breathe, my body still tried to make it seem important, and hyperventilating still hurt.

I felt like I was being strangled by the dark, by my clothes—*and what is that awful weight on my back*? I clawed at the dark, and even at my own skin, until I could feel the straps and bits of cloth and get free of all of it.

It was only once I was mostly naked, and was able to take a full deep breath, that I realized this was probably not the most ideal place to be unclothed exposed. However, I was no longer freaking out as badly. I was blindly sorting through the things I had ripped off, when I realized the crushing weight I had felt was my backpack. What was in that backpack? Yep: the flashlight.

I pulled out the heavy cylindrical object and flipped it on, anxious for the comfort of a light in the dark. The darkness sprang to life in front of me in ways I couldn't have imagined—and it was horrible.

The things I saw were burned into my brain, even though I only viewed them for a split second before turning the light back off. I couldn't find Raphael without the light—couldn't move out of this spot without the light. I was a sitting target if I didn't move, and I was a moving target with the light on.

I was so out of my league. I knew with all certainty now that I really wasn't going to make it out of here. Going back the way I came wasn't an option, so giving up now would be pointless. I resolved myself to at least find Raphael before I was captured by Lucifer or one of his demons.

A few of the nightmarish images I had seen nudged me to reconsider as I got ready to turn my light back on. I knew there was no way to avoid the things I would have to see and face. I told myself maybe it was all an illusion—just tricks set up to spook me. *It's not real*, I said to myself. And as I clicked on my flashlight and let myself take in all the nightmares of the room, I just kept repeating my new mantra over, and over, and over again.

CHAPTER FOURTEEN

I couldn't tell if I was in a room, or cave. Without my light, it was blackness, but even with it, there were no walls or ceiling that I could see. I shined my light up and it seemed to go too high, until the light of my flashlight was lost in the dark beyond it. I knew I hadn't fallen so far.

I decided to move forward, passing by things that one part of my mind wanted to try to make sense of, but the other part wouldn't allow.

There were strings, and wires—contraptions of all sorts. There were faces frozen in expressions I didn't want to understand, and things added or missing where other body parts should have been.

I tried not to look, but they were everywhere. The more I saw, the more I believed the mantra I was chanting—there was no way these were real people. They couldn't be dead, and there was no screaming, no blood. It was just for shock-value.

Once fear no longer had the upper hand, I moved much faster. I half walked, half jogged—still too cautious to break out into a full run—and I was trying to listen as I went. It was so quiet here, at least in the part of Hell that I was in.

I remembered the copy of Dante's *Inferno* that was on our bookshelf in the cabin. I'd first read it at fourteen, and then again around twenty. It was a book that had stayed with me through the years. Even though I wasn't religious, I was always fascinated by the beliefs of people about what happened to us after death.

Now, walking through Hell, I wondered if there was any accuracy to Dante's book. *Am I walking through the second circle of Hell, perhaps?* If that was how this worked, I really hoped that Raphael was in one of the first few levels.

I didn't realize how lost I was in my own thoughts, until my skin began to tingle and goosebumps ran along my arms. Trying to notice what was different, I stopped to take in my surroundings. I rubbed my head and came away with sweat—not a small amount of sweat, either. I was soaked. My body was trying so hard to cool itself down, that was what caused the goosebumps. The heat must have been increasing incredibly slowly for me not to notice the temperature shift until now.

A sound caught my attention. It was the first thing that I had heard down here besides my own breathing. The things around me weren't alive, so it had to be coming from somewhere in the distance. I wanted to run towards the sound, towards another person who could possibly help me.

Hades's voice echoed in my head, reminding me to be wary of demons. I wasn't sure what a demon would look like, but I was pretty sure I'd know when I saw one.

The sound changed in tone: sometimes it was louder,

and sometimes more distant, but it was a constant sound. As I went along, trusting my ears and feet to take me in the right direction, I noticed an orange-red glow in the darkness. It became brighter and brighter until my flashlight was no longer needed. I clicked off the light and put it back in the pocket of my backpack. Excited to at least move into a different area, I let myself increase my speed, making sure to still move as silently as I could.

My clothes clung to me as if I had showered in them, and I knew that my body was hot because of how much I was sweating, but I didn't feel the heat like I should've been able to.

The glow was even brighter now, and I couldn't tell if it was fire I was seeing, or just the light from another place. It captivated my sight and I ran towards it, no longer looking down at where my feet were landing.

Even as the light got brighter, I felt like I had been running for ages, and I briefly wondered if this was another trick, like the brimstone. *Will I run forever and never get there?*

My question was answered as my right foot went down, and suddenly there was nothing under it. I was about to run off of a cliff. My body was already moving forward to take me down, and it took every ounce of my strength to halt that momentum. I screamed, and managed to throw my body backwards to keep from plummeting over the edge. My legs were dangling off the ledge, and my head smacked hard on the ground as I went down, filling with pounding, searing pain that reminded far too much of the way I had died.

I blinked as I saw fire shoot up from the pit below, and heard the popping, sizzling sound as flames licked at the bottoms of my boots. I knew I should move, but I couldn't. Then darkness pulled me back in, as the pain became too much to bear.

My head still pounded as I came to. My arms ached above my head, and I tried to put them back down by my sides, only to find I couldn't make them move. My legs were straight, no longer hanging over the edge of the fiery pit, but they were a bit farther apart than was comfortable. I found I couldn't move them either.

I opened my eyes and once again found myself in darkness. I turned my head from left to right, and felt the movement of cloth against my face; it was dark because there was some kind of bag over my head.

The back of my body was pressed against something that didn't feel like the ground I had been on earlier, and the sensation wasn't lessened by clothing. It was my bare skin against whatever surface I was on.

My heart pounded, and immediately I fought against my restraints. I'd been captured.

"I wouldn't pull too hard on those restraints, there, Miss," a man said. He spoke with a British accent, but not the kind that sounded refined: the kind that sounded heavy with alcohol, and wore clothes that hadn't been washed in some time.

"Right, you wouldn't want to hurt yourself," another man chuckled. There was nothing distinct about his voice.

"Don't want you doing our job for us!" the Brit replied, and the two men laughed heartily.

I froze: I didn't speak, move, or breathe. These had

to be demons.

"We haven't been able to figure out who you are, or how you got here," the plain sounding man said. "We were just making our rounds and found you out by the pit. I wanted to just toss you in and be done with it, but Zeke over here said we shouldn't waste you like that."

The Brit, whom I now knew as Zeke, spoke up. "We never get to have much fun—'e always sticks us with patrolling the outer areas. But he's away right now, and you were just too pretty to pass up."

I could only assume the "he" Zeke referred to was Lucifer.

I thought about telling them Lucifer had given me the OK to come down here and retrieve Raphael's soul, but I doubted they would believe me. I thought about arguing that I wasn't a bad person and didn't belong here. I was sure that would be original.

No, I had read about torture. There were only ever two good reasons for torture: To get information, and for sadistic pleasure. I didn't have any information to share, therefore it was the second, which was much worse. They just wanted to see my pain and get a reaction out of me. I thought about trying to ignore whatever they were going to do to me, and die again before I made even a peep; but they knew everyone screamed eventually, and would just hurt me worse, faster. Or I could act like I was in agony from the first touch, and hope they never stepped up the intensity. That seemed like such a coward's choice, but I didn't see that it really mattered if I was brave right now.

I felt something brush the side of my ribcage, and I screamed—not from pain, but just from the surprise.

"Oy, Jake. She's a jumpy one! This'll be fun," Zeke said.

"Are you not going to talk to us?" Jake asked, and I assumed he must be talking to me.

I remained still and silent.

"Well, you don't have to talk to us, it's OK," he said in the voice you'd use to comfort a crying child.

And then I felt one of them touch me again, and I started screaming.

CHAPTER FIFTEEN

I DIDN'T REALIZE HOW FAST VOCAL CHORDS GAVE out. My screaming like a banshee at every little poke and pinch had backfired after what seemed like a fairly short amount of time.

They hadn't raped me, and for that I was thankful. Being naked and left at the hands of demons, I knew things could get so much worse.

I did feel like a strange science experiment. It was like they were asking, *What sound does she make if we use this tool, and touch her here? Now what happens there?*

I wasn't physically capable of even making noises now, unless something was shocking or painful—which the demons interpreted as them needing to do worse things.

The bag was still over my face, and I jumped every time I felt one of them come closer. I didn't know if it would make it better or worse to see what was coming next.

"Let's get the needles," Jake said.

"No, the knives," Zeke argued.

I had a feeling if I threw in my suggestion it would be used against me, so again, I said nothing—not that

I could have said anything anyway.

"We need to pace ourselves," Jake told Zeke. "If we start with knives, she'll lose consciousness again, and then we can't play."

"Or..." Zeke started as his vile idea formed, "we could just go for it and see what 'appens. I know we wouldn't get to play as long, but we never get to do the really fun stuff."

"What were you thinking?" Jake asked with piqued interest.

"Set up the bar, and I'll grab the hooks," Zeke said with way too much excitement in his voice. "The knives are already out here."

I couldn't listen anymore, couldn't think about the horrors awaiting me. I drifted off to memories of home, digging in my cemetery, watching over the graves... cooking in the cabin with Ray, and of course, meeting Raphael.

I asked myself if he was worth it. Knowing where my infatuation with him had led me, to this very moment, *Would I still do things the same?* I wanted to answer that I would, and that Brandon probably would have killed me anyway, but I wasn't really sure anymore. *Is one person, any person who isn't your own child, worth the eternal torture of your soul?*

There was the clanging of metal near me, and I jumped back to the present.

"Make sure it's together good. We don't want it falling apart when we get her up there," Jake said.

"'Ave you done this before?" Zeke asked, sounding a little less self-assured this time.

"Nah, but I've watched others do it plenty," Jake said.

"Doesn't it take three people?" Zeke asked.

"Shit, yeah it does, unless one of the guys is really strong—'cause two people have to hold them up while other person gets the hooks in just right," Jake replied.

Hanging by hooks… I swallowed hard. *Why did I think I could do this?*

"Let's go get one of the bigger guys to help us, just in case," Zeke suggested. "I just don't want to fuck it up."

Apparently that's what they had decided to do, because I heard them walk away. I struggled at the ropes again, and moved my head violently until I managed to get the hood off. The lighting was dim so it didn't take more than a few seconds for my eyes to adjust. I looked down the line of my naked, bruised body, and sighed.

Just a few feet away was a table set up with the tools and torture implements they had used (or were planning to use) on me. On the other side was what I could only compare to a heavy duty clothes rack, with large, sharp metal hooks over the top bar. I thought of feeling those hooks sink into my flesh, and it made me gag.

I pulled harder than ever on the restraints, and could see now that the restraints were made from tiny wires made into a flexible metal rope. The wires scratched and pinched and cut into my skin, feeling like I had scrubbed it raw with a combination of steel wool and insulation.

A soft sob escaped my lips, and I bit my tongue until I tasted blood to quiet myself. They would be back any minute with another demon. If I had any hope of escape, this might be it. I thought of Grace and Ray and all of my friends, and promised myself that if I got away, I would get back to them, Raphael or no Raphael. I would break my wrists, if I had to, to get out of these restraints. But my arms were stretched to their max, and no matter how I moved, I couldn't get the right leverage to pull hard enough.

"Look at you, trying to be all sneaky," Jake said.

Zeke made a "tsk-tsk" sound, and shook his finger at me.

They didn't seem to care that I could see them now. I, however, was shocked to see that both of my tormentors were, pardon the expression, but, "sexy as Hell." Never having been good at hiding my emotions, the demons regarded my shock with amusement.

"Never seen a demon before?" Jake asked. His skin was the color of dark chocolate, and his eyes were pale jade green; braids hung down his back, and he was shirtless.

"Well, you're certainly not what I expected a demon to look like," I said, breaking my long silence. My voice had already started to recover, since it had been a few minutes since I had last screamed; my throat still felt scratchy, though.

These two had sounded like bumbling idiots while I was under that hood. If these were the lesser demons, I wondered what the important ones looked like. Of course, more important didn't necessarily mean prettier or smarter—just like they didn't have to be the brightest bulbs in order to hurt me, and look good while they did it.

Zeke stepped a little closer and grinned. He was no less appealing than his friend, though not quite as tall; Zeke had pretty blue eyes that reminded me of new denim jeans. He was built like a boxer, with a gristly upper body, short brown hair, and a five o'clock shadow. He looked young and feisty, and if I hadn't just been tortured by them, I might have flirted.

"Demons get a bad wrap for being ugly and monstrous, but those are a particular type of demon: the ones that possess people. They are ugly little fuckers," Zeke said.

"Just waiting for our help, and we'll get started," Jake assured me, like I was being impatient.

They didn't seem to dislike me. This wasn't personal: it was just what they knew—what they did. I understood that, but it didn't make me feel any better about what was coming next.

I heard the other demon's footsteps coming towards us. I looked over at the metal rack and hooks awaiting me. I closed my eyes and tried to remind myself that this wasn't going to kill me, it would only hurt, and pain never lasts forever.

"Have you flayed the arms yet?" I heard the new guy ask.

I shut my eyes tight to keep the room from spinning; my stomach turned, and I fought not to throw up.

"Please don't," I squeaked. I never imagined myself as the kind of person who would beg sadistic torturers for mercy (which was very stupid), but I couldn't help myself.

The new demon had his back to me, and stood farther away than the other two. I saw the glint of a silver blade as he held it up to examine the shape and sharpness. At my pathetic plea, he turned around and walked over to me. My eyes were unfocused with fear, and the shadows that filled the room, so I didn't see that it was Raphael until he was leaning directly over me, searching my face. His hair was pulled back in a ponytail so that his face was clean and defined. Like the other demons, he wore black pants and no shirt—and his eyes, those deep ocean blue eyes I wanted to drown in, were staring directly into mine. He was still the most beautiful man I had ever seen.

I knew my eyes widened when I realized it was him, but I didn't know if I should call him by his name, or make it known that I knew him. His face stayed completely unreadable as he stood over me, and I had no idea whether or not he recognized me. How long had it even been at this point?

He narrowed his deep blue eyes at me, and held the knife just in front of my face. "Please don't," he repeated, mocking my words and the sound of my voice. "If we don't open your arms up, how are we supposed to hang you up by your tendons and ligaments?"

I managed to turn my head just enough to miss vomiting on both of us. Hot tears streamed down my face, and I refused to say another word. I closed my eyes and turned my head away from Raphael, unable to watch if he was really going to hurt me in such a way.

"Let me do it," Zeke said, sounding like a little kid who wanted a turn playing with the big boys. He held out his hand for the knife.

"Well if he gets to do one arm, I want to do the other," Jake chimed in.

This is not the way I fantasized about three sexy men fighting over me.

Raphael hesitated for a moment, and then handed

the knife over to Zeke. My heart sank.

I felt the tip of the knife pierce the tender flesh just below my hand, and I gasped. Quickly I bit down on my lip to keep from letting myself make another sound. Fuck the pain, I wouldn't give them the satisfaction of one more whimper.

The knife cut through my skin easily, but not painlessly. Tears flowed down my face and dripped off of my chin.

"Wait," Raphael said, and Zeke stopped cutting, but still left the blade under my skin. "Where are your plans to catch the blood? You know if Lucifer finds out you did this and didn't at least save her blood for an offering…" He trailed off, letting them imagine the consequences for themselves.

I opened one eye to see what was going on. Jake and Zeke looked concerned.

"Yeah, man, he's right. We need to get a pan," Jake agreed.

"I'll stay here and make sure she doesn't escape, and hold pressure on the wound until you get back. That way none of it is wasted," Raphael assured them.

I stared at him, wondering who he was helping. He didn't look at me once, so I tried not to get my hopes up.

The other two demons cursed, and Zeke wiped my blood off of his hands on a nearby towel.

"We'll be back as soon as we can," Jake told us.

"Go to the lower pits—their pans are less likely to spill," Raphael suggested.

Zeke nodded, and off they went.

Raphael had wrapped a towel around my wrist, and was holding it tightly so that my apparently precious blood didn't splatter on the floor. Once the other demons were out of sight, he looked around to make sure we were alone.

"Hel," he whispered looking down at me. He leaned in quickly and his mouth was on mine. I growled and turned away from him, terrified.

He pulled back and held his hands up in front of himself to show he meant no harm. His face showed total horror and embarrassment, and he gasped, "Oh God, I'm so sorry! Of course you didn't want me to kiss you. I was just so happy to see you. Can I get you out of here?"

Even I had been surprised at my violent reaction to his kiss. I had wanted him to kiss me, more than anything I'd ever wanted in my life, before today—before I found out he was a demon. Now I wasn't sure I wanted him to touch me; but the others would be back, and my chance would be gone.

"Get me out of here," I said.

CHAPTER SIXTEEN

"I HAVE TO TOUCH YOU TO GET YOU LOOSE. IT might hurt," he warned.

I nodded in understanding, and my eyes followed his movements as he undid the restraint on one arm. I only winced for a second, but that was my good arm. As he moved to the one with the wound, I whimpered, and knew my face didn't hide the pain that ran through me.

"I am so sorry," he said, as he freed my wrist and tied the towel back around it.

I didn't know what to say to him, so I sat up and started working to get my ankle free from the next set of restraints; Raphael worked on the other.

Once I was free, he stood in front of me and offered me his hands to help me off of the table where I had been laying for so long.

Reluctantly, I put my hands in his and let him help me stand. I hated that I was naked, but not once did Raphael's eyes wander away from my eyes while he was helping me, and if they did, it was only to assess my injuries.

My legs gave way the moment my weight was on

them. I came crashing down nearly to the floor before Raphael's arms caught me.

"You'll have to let me carry you," he said.

I shook my head adamantly. "No."

"I understand, and once I have you somewhere safe, you don't ever have to see or speak to me again, if you hate me. But Hel, I lost you once to a really bad person. Don't make me watch it happen again." Raphael's eyes were full of pain.

"OK," I said, and wrapped my arms around his neck as he scooped me up. I fought the urge to put my head on his shoulder as he carried me. I thought about what he said. *Do I hate him? Is it even possible for me to hate him?*

I didn't have a clue where we were in relation to where I came in, or even where I had fallen. It wasn't totally dark down here, but it wasn't far off. Hell glowed like smoldering coals left in the fireplace, with areas of darkness and pinpoints of hot light.

I recognized the pit I had almost tumbled into as we walked by it, and the flames jumped to life again. I wondered if Lucifer had it on a motion-sensor, or if it was a natural cycle, like a geyser.

Embers flew in front of my eyes, and I ducked my face in against Raphael's neck. He held me even more tightly, and whispered to me, "Shh, I won't let anything else hurt you, I promise."

Tired and still in pain, I finally let my head rest on his shoulder, my lips lightly touching his neck, and I breathed him in. It had been so long since I had known the safety of his arms, since I had smelled the sweetness of his skin. I let out a long relaxed breath, and felt him sigh.

In this moment, I didn't care what he was or how he came to be here. He was still my Raphael: the one I had risked everything to find.

A quiet laugh escaped my lips.

Raphael looked down at me as he continued to carry me. "What could possibly be amusing right now?"

"I came here to rescue you," I chuckled.

I saw the smile spread across his face and reach his eyes. "Did you really?"

I nuzzled his neck. "Yep. I never stopped trying to find you." I yawned, "How much farther until we're in your safe place?"

"Just a little ways to go, sweetheart. Just rest," he soothed.

I couldn't believe I wanted to sleep. I wasn't out of danger yet, and the towel around my arm was wet with my blood. Raphael was carrying me through Hell, and yet, I slept.

I had vague memories of a hidden room, and Raphael gently laying me down on the bed. Sleep held me tightly for a long while, but when it finally let me out of its grasp, I opened my eyes and found myself looking into Raphael's.

"Hi, there," I smiled, feeling much more like myself than in the previous hours.

"Hi," he said, with a smile to rival my own.

"Where are we?" I asked.

"Just a little room I found down below the pit. Most of the other demons don't know it's here, and when the flames are burning you can't even see it," he assured me.

"So we're safe?"

He nodded.

I didn't feel safe. *What happens when we want to leave this room?* I had so many questions for him, I didn't know where to start.

He touched my face, and looked relieved when I didn't flinch or pull away. "My Hel," he said softly as he stroked my hair. "Did you really come here to save me?" He sounded so surprised. "How did you know where I was, and how did you get here?"

Apparently he had as many questions for me as I did for him.

I wiggled my body in closer to his. "We're safe for a while?" I asked once more, ignoring all of his questions.

His breathing was suddenly more controlled, and his eyes were locked on mine. "Yes, until we leave this room."

I had him—I had him back with me. Even if it was only for a little while, I had found him and he was here with me now, and what happened after this was something to worry about another time. I leaned in and gently pressed my lips to his.

He tensed, but didn't move. He let me kiss him, but didn't touch me or kiss me back.

I pulled back just enough to say, "It's OK, I want you."

This time when I kissed him, he opened his mouth to me and wrapped his arms around my back, gently holding me and rubbing my skin.

I was suddenly aware I was still naked, as his fingertips traced my curves underneath the soft blanket.

I couldn't decide if I wanted to push him away, or if I couldn't get all of him against me fast enough.

This time he pulled back and looked at me. "Are you sure you want to do this, with me, here?"

The first time we had ever made love was at my cabin. He had been just as sweet and considerate then, asking me what I wanted, if I was OK—making sure I felt safe and comfortable with everything that we did together.

"Yes. I've never been more certain of anything," I said.

Raphael kissed my mouth like he was starving and I was his favorite food. He kissed every scratch and bruise that the other demons had left on my body.

When my mind tried to guess why Raphael was a demon, I pushed those thoughts far, far away, and told them they could come back later.

By the time he was finished kissing all of the areas he wanted to kiss, my body was a wet, writhing mess.

"Enough!" I gasped as his face emerged from underneath the blanket. He kissed my mouth, and I could taste myself on his lips and tongue. For some people that was repulsive, but I found to be a huge turn on. I felt the same way when a guy pulled me in for a passionate kiss after I had been going down on him. I understood how it might bother germaphobes, but I tended to enjoy the kinky, dirty parts of sex.

"You have to be inside me, right now," I demanded in a voice nearly breathless with need.

"I wanted to stretch this out, enjoy as long as we can," Raphael said, the tip of him pressed against me—he was teasing.

I shook my head. "I have been waiting for you much too long for that. We can go slow next time." I wrapped my arms around his neck and pushed my hips up towards his. "I need you, Raphael."

He slid inside of me a little deeper and faster than I was prepared for, and I cried out against his chest, digging the fingers of my uninjured hand into his back.

"I've been needing you for so long," he said.

I was snuggled in against Raphael's chest, wrapped around his body so that every part of me was touching some part of him. I had been without him for much too long. In life, I had never been the clingy type, but if he wanted rid of me now he'd have to pry me off with a crowbar, and I told him so.

He had laughed a sincere, rich sound. "I don't think either of us will need any alone time for a long while. Be as clingy as you want to be."

We laid in silence a while, and then he said, "Tell me everything I missed."

"Starting when?" I asked. "When I died?"

He shook his head and sniffed. When I looked up at him, he was crying.

"Raphael," I touched his face.

"No, not that. I still can't bear it. I was so close and couldn't save you." He was still shaking his head.

It wasn't my favorite day to talk about either, but in no way could I have blamed him for all the things that went wrong the day I died. So I told him about waking up in the field, and pretty much everything that had happened since. I left out the fact that I'd sought comfort in the arms of Boude, and my strange relationship with Soren. That wasn't pertinent right now.

"You dug me up when I died?" he asked.

"I did," I took a shaky breath, "and I lost you all over again."

He hugged me tightly. "After all that, you still looked for me."

We hadn't said it, even though I was pretty sure we had both felt it from the first night we met. "Of course. I love you," I told him.

He kissed the top of my head, and then my lips. "I love you too."

CHAPTER SEVENTEEN

I HAD NEVER BEEN SO HAPPY TO HEAR THOSE WORDS. As much as I loved Raphael, there was always a part of me that was scared that he didn't feel the same way. Knowing now that he did, that he wanted me just as much as I wanted him, I thought my heart would burst.

"I want to know everything that happened with you after I died," I told him. We were on our sides face to face. I was playing with his long black hair, twisting it through my fingers. "Actually, after I was buried. I don't want to hear about the pain my death caused you." I closed my eyes, fighting back a few tears.

He rubbed my arm as he spoke. "Well, I left. I went out west and took pictures, and tried to find anyone who could tell me why the people I loved kept dying, or leaving. I saw psychics, and shamans, and people who did all kinds of strange things. Most were con artists, but a few were insightful, talking about souls, and how sometimes a soul couldn't complete its true mission in the world of the living. Sometimes karma had to be paid in death itself, or in the afterlife. He said people who are surrounded by death in such a way are being prepared for what's to come." Raphael's voice was steady as he told me the story.

"That's not creepy at all," I interrupted.

He nodded, and continued, "It wasn't long after that meeting that I died. My heart just stopped—I felt it. I don't know if there was some underlying medical reason it quit on me so young… or if I had just hurt too much for it to stand."

"I'm so sorry," I told him.

He kissed me. "I'm not." Raphael went on, "The next thing I knew I was wandering around these lush green fields talking to people who were just as lost as me. I was there for a while, and it was peaceful." There was longing in his eyes.

I finally asked him the question I wanted to ask, and dreaded to ask. "Raphael, how did you get here? How did you become a demon?"

He bit his lip and looked away from me, blinking back a few tears. "I was walking by myself, something I did all the time, and a man came up to me from out of nowhere. He wasn't very tall, but wore glasses and fedora; he had a deep accent, and a strange name."

"Thaddeus Broche," I said.

Raphael's eyes widened. "That was it! He told me I was sent to that place by mistake, and he was there to take me back to the right part of the underworld. He told me someone was waiting for me. You were the only person I could think it might be, but I didn't want to get my hopes up," he smiled. "He told me about how a crazy vampire had messed with a lot of souls and sent them to the wrong places, and said that's what had happened to me. He told me he had to make a few stops as we went along to collect more souls to take back. He said he had already taken a few back to the main area of the underworld, but that it was taking too long to make that many trips. So we went in and out of several different afterlives. Most of the gods weren't pleasant about the misunderstanding, but didn't want to keep souls with no desire to serve them. They turned over the souls, and we were on our way." He sighed. "Hell was supposed to be our last stop. Negotiations were taking longer than expected, since Lucifer didn't care if the souls had been sent to him by mistake, and Thaddeus knew he would be in trouble if he returned without all of the lost souls. We were safe, or so we thought, waiting in an abandoned area for Thaddeus to take us where we belonged. There were maybe a hundred or so souls. Then Thaddeus didn't return from his meeting with Lucifer. A bunch of demons came in and captured everyone. We were told Thaddeus had been called away suddenly and was unable to take us with him. The way Lucifer saw it, we were his now."

Raphael stopped for moment, and I watched him shudder as he recalled what happened next.

"We were given options: we could join him; we could remain prisoners, open to whatever sadistic fun the demons wanted to have with us, in hopes that we might one day be rescued; or we could jump into the pit and let our souls be burned up forever—true death." He blinked and looked away. "More than you would have thought made that last choice."

I imagined watching people purposefully jump into the pit of fire to meet their end, so they didn't have to endure or inflict torment for eternity. I did understand their choice, but I didn't think I could have made the same one; no matter how bleak things were, I had always tried to hold on to that spark of hope.

"You joined him," I said. There was no judgment in my voice; there were no "good" choices to make in that situation. I wouldn't have condemned him for any of them.

"I'm a coward," he said, and I saw so much anguish on his face. "I've tortured people so that I didn't have to endure the pain myself," he said.

"I don't believe for moment that you aren't torturing yourself."

He rolled his eyes and wiped away a few tears. "I've grown cold to it—I don't even hear the screams anymore."

I pictured Raphael standing over someone strapped to a table, like I had been, covered in their blood, numb to their suffering. It should have scared me—it should have broken my heart. I hated it, but I was just so glad I had found him—glad he had saved me.

"You aren't a monster, Raphael. You did what you had to do to get through this," I reassured him.

"I'm not the same person you knew, Hel."

"I'm not either," I said. "But let's figure out how to get out of here, and we can get to know one another again."

Raphael went still beside me and didn't say anything.

"What?" I searched his face, and asked, "Will we ever be able to get out of here?" while questions like, *Are we just delaying the inevitable? Are we going to have to jump into the pit to escape this place?* ran through my mind.

"I will find a way to get you out of here, I promise,"

he said.

"What do you mean, 'get *you* out of here?' You have to come with me, or I'm not going." I awkwardly crossed my arms across my chest and winced. *Stupid bandage.*

"Helena, the things I've done are too awful. This is where I deserve to be now."

"Bullshit. If you stay, you'll just end up doing more bad things. Stop it, you are coming back with me." This was not up for discussion. "If I leave here without you, this was all for nothing. Do you really want that?"

He rolled onto his back and rubbed his face. I sat up and leaned over him. "Do you want me to have been tortured for nothing?"

He opened his eyes. "Of course not, but how I can face others knowing the horrible things I've done to people?"

I shrugged. "I can't answer that, but you won't figure out how to make it better by staying here where it all happened, and will most likely happen again."

He pulled me down to lay on top of him, and I kissed along his neck and collar bone. He sighed, and squeezed me. "Getting out of here is going to be tough. Whenever Hades opened all the doors, Lucifer had this one sealed back up in seconds, but a few managed to escape anyway. I'm sure he put up extra precautions to make leaving even more difficult now."

"Do you know of any ways to get out—at all?" I asked.

"I've heard that in his personal chambers, there's a hidden door or way out."

"I'm guessing even getting inside there is almost impossible," I surmised.

"It is heavily guarded by high-level demons."

"Of course it is," I said. "Is it dangerous here for you now? I mean Jake and Zeke know you helped me escape. Will the other demons be looking for you?"

He shrugged. "Eh, I can handle them. I'll just say you told me who you were, and that you were sent by Hades to discuss a matter with Lucifer, and I had to let you go."

"Will they believe that?"

"As far as they know, I'd have no reason to let you go. I'm just as sadistic as they are, remember?" Raphael gave a half-hearted laugh that didn't sound amused at all.

He had been playing the role of a sadist, and I tried not to cringe too hard thinking about the fate he had saved me from. A part of my brain kept repeating, *But he did do that to other people.* I tried to find any other thought to focus on, but that one insisted on being heard. Sometimes fighting the bad thoughts and painful memories made it worse. If you could stand it, and just let it play through, it might go away for a little longer.

Raphael put his hand on top of mine. I had been absentmindedly rubbing the bandage around my wrist. Little streaks of crimson had blossomed on the white cloth.

"Shit," I said, "I reopened it. I wasn't thinking."

Raphael sat up and took my arm in his lap. Gently, he unwrapped the rags he had used, and wiped away the fresh blood.

I had to look away to keep from getting sick. I'd never been good with blood, which most people found strange for the amount of dead bodies I had seen. But the corpses I dealt with had been embalmed: no blood, no mess.

"How bad is it?" I asked him.

"Zeke cut deeper than he needed just to skin your arm. Idiot," he breathed as he looked more closely.

I fought my gag reflex at the "skin your arm" comment. I hated that I knew what they were planning to do to me; I hated worse that Raphael was the one who told me. I heard it again in my head like I was back on the table, "If we don't open your arms up, how are we supposed to hang you up by your tendons and ligaments?"

Instinctively, I jerked my arm out of his grasp and cradled it to me, not caring that I was getting blood all over my chest.

The surprise on Raphael's face was clear. "Did I hurt you?" he said, placing a hand on my leg.

I took a slow breath, and was quite embarrassed I had acted that way, like he would hurt me. I knew that he wouldn't, that he had to fake it in front of the other demons in order to get a chance to save me. I still couldn't help that those words stung, on a deep level. And at the time, I hadn't been sure that they were lies.

I knew that telling him what was wrong would hurt him. One of us hurting was enough. "Yeah, sorry," I said, placing my arm back in his hands, "it just really hurt for second."

"Sorry, baby. He probably got a couple of nerves." Raphael rewrapped my wrist with a clean cloth. "Try to keep it still. It would have been better if we could have stitched it, but you don't want to keep tearing it open."

I looked at my arm, and the cloth he had wrapped

with so much care. "Thank you," I said, and leaned in to kiss him.

"You're welcome," he said, and kissed my lips, then my forehead.

"Now what?" I asked.

"Now we need to try to get out of here, and into the Devil's bedroom," he said with a grin I wasn't expecting.

"Why are you smiling? We might not make it through this."

"If we don't, we'll die together; and if we do, we'll have a fucking awesome story to tell."

I shook my head at him—but if those were our only choices, I'd take them.

CHAPTER EIGHTEEN

We didn't make it far out of our hidden paradise. Hell was crawling with demons, all looking for Raphael and me.

I was right when I suspected that Zeke and Jake would run their mouths to everyone about how Raphael had betrayed them and escaped with a prisoner. Raphael had immediately given his spiel about how I was there as a messenger from Hades, and how Lucifer would be upset if I was tortured. Most of the demons thought he was lying, but enough of them found it feasible enough not to haul me off and finish what they started.

They put Raphael on his knees and bound his hands behind his back with the same awful wire rope they'd used on me. He was smart enough not to test it's give. They made me get on my knees beside him, but didn't tie my hands. I guess I didn't seem very threatening.

When I say a lot of demons were looking for us, I wasn't just referring to the pretty ones. As I looked around, I saw horns of varying lengths, growing not just from their heads, but from various areas of their bodies. On some there were snouts where noses should have been, and fangs snarled at me from otherwise beautiful faces. A clip-clopping sound made me look for the source, and I saw three or four creatures walking up on cloven-hooved goat's legs. The ones that bothered me the most, though, were the ones crawling on their bellies, with arms and legs so close to their bodies that I thought they were slithering at first. Their faces were almost childlike, with chubby cheeks and full round lips; some had hair, and others were bald, only increasing the resemblance to infants. One crawled up to me, and to my horror, it stuck out a forked snake's tongue and *tasted* me. Thankful to at least be wearing a long shirt Raphael had given me, I still jerked back, almost falling over in my unstable position on the ground. The child/snake demon rolled its eyes up to look at me, and smiled before going back to its fellows.

"So what do we do with them?" a demon that I couldn't see asked from somewhere in the crowd.

Most of the suggestions were not things we would enjoy, but that wasn't surprising.

"No!" a woman's voice roared. "They will go before the Prince, and be judged how he sees fit."

I saw a woman walking forward, and the crowd parted for her, with room to spare. She was important, and everyone knew it.

All of the muscles in Raphael's jaw and shoulder clenched, and he looked at the ground. The woman stood tall, and seemed to notice Raphael's discomfort with her.

She was lovely, with brown skin, and long golden-brown hair. Her ankle length red dress fit her well, and delicate gold chains hung from her neck and wrists.

As she walked up to Raphael, I could see he was trying to steady himself, trying not to flinch or pull back from her.

"Raphael, what have you gotten yourself into since the last time I visited, hmm?" she asked. She paced in slow deliberate circles around him, like a shark deciding if it was going to take a bite.

He caught my gaze, and must have noticed my worried expression; a look of apology filled his eyes, and then he turned his attention back to her. I saw something new come over him. He straightened his back, and instead of flinching, he smiled at her and made eye contact.

"Lamashtu, you know I'm not one to start trouble." He grinned at her and blinked those lovely eyes.

She stopped pacing in front of him, and cupped his face in the palm of her hand. "I certainly hope you haven't done something stupid." She traced her fingertips across his lips. "I would hate to lose my favorite lover." She winked, and made a kissing sound at him.

Raphael dropped his head, but kept his eyes on hers—perfect bedroom eyes.

Demon or not, I was pissed now.

"You know, it would get me back in your bed faster if you could vouch for me in front of Lucifer. We have spent quite a bit of time together," he teased.

"I would like to have you back in my bed," she said, as if she was considering his proposal. Then she turned on her bare feet and slapped him so hard his body swayed and he had to blink multiple times to clear his head. "I vouch for no one in front of our dark prince. You either make it on your own merit, or you don't. That's how I've survived these thousand years." She almost left it at that, but then added, "And yes, Raphael, you have a very nice dick, but it can be replaced. Or if he no longer has a use for you, I'll just take yours as a souvenir before you're thrown into the pit." Lamashtu gave us one more smile and stepped back.

I noticed Raphael giving me an unfriendly glare, and that's when I realized I had been smiling. *Oops*. I hated knowing they had been lovers, and I hated listening to him bait her, but damn, she had handled herself well. I erased the grin from my face, and pretended instead that I had been horrified by all of it.

Getting back to the situation at hand, Zeke pointed out, "Lucifer is away from us right now. What do we do with them until he gets back?"

"Sounds like I chose the perfect time to check back in," a new voice said.

Knees dropped and heads bowed in unison as he walked through the crowd. I saw that Raphael's head was down, so I put mine down as well, even though I really wanted to look up to see if he still looked like Raphael.

"Lamashtu, tell me what's been going on here," he ordered.

"My Prince, Zeke and Jake found this woman unconscious by the pit. They decided to enjoy her company and offer her blood as a sacrifice to you. They asked Raphael for help. When they left her alone with him for a short period of time, he released her, and they've been in hiding together. However, Raphael claims he only released her because she was sent here by Hades with a message to you," she finished.

I couldn't take it. I raised my head to look at Lucifer, hoping he wasn't still sharing the same skin as my lover. He wasn't: his hair was lighter now, and his eyes were brown. He looked like any average man walking down the street of any American suburb. Watching these powerful demonic creatures kneel before him was strange. If I hadn't seen their reaction to him, I wouldn't have known this was Satan. How did they?

"I see," he said as he looked at us. Then he snapped his fingers at the female demon. "Prepare my chamber for us. I feel like there is more to this that we're not being told." He half smiled at me.

Lamashtu nodded, and hurried off to do as he asked.

I had the feeling his chamber wasn't being prepared for a sleepover. He knew exactly what was going on here—I wondered why he was pretending he didn't. He could have us tortured either way, on his word alone.

Raphael told me not to look around as we were led through all of Hell to the home of the devil himself. I heard strange noises, and the movements I caught sight of in my periphery were frightening, to say the least. I was already terrified.

I desperately wanted to be holding Raphael's hand—after all, these might be our last moments together.

The path we walked on seemed to spiral down, and down, and down into the very center of Hell. A door stood where the path ended, and I could only assume this was our destination.

I had wanted the long death march to end, but now

I was wishing the road had been even longer.

As the demon escorting us knocked on the large wooden door, I looked over at Raphael. The door had already started to open when I saw his lips move to soundlessly say, "I love you."

Before I could respond, we were being ushered inside.

The room was large and dark, and strangely cozier and less creepy than Rasputin's bedroom back at the mansion. That realization bothered me.

A large high-backed chair sat in the middle of the room, in front of a roaring fireplace made of large stones. Plush rugs lined the floor, and candles burned in sconces on the walls.

I didn't see any actual doors in the room, but shadowed doorways were tucked away in the corners. I wondered if one led to his bedroom—*but does the devil need to sleep?*

Lucifer stepped out from one of the dark hallways and smiled, with a look that said he knew that he could do absolutely anything he wanted to us.

"You may go," he said to the demon with us.

"But, my Prince, I…" The devil held up his hand, stopping him mid-sentence.

"You may go," he said again, but this time the look in his eyes wasn't as friendly.

I didn't think it was a good sign that he didn't want anyone else with us.

The guard left, and Lucifer paced around the room. Raphael and I said nothing, but stood close enough to touch, side by side.

"So, you rescued your man, I see." Lucifer laughed. "Well you tried!" he shrugged.

I dropped my head; I was well aware that I had failed us both.

"Excellent effort, though, very impressive, daughter of mine," he smiled.

"I'm not your daughter." My tone was thick with the horror of the thought.

"Oh but you are!" he cheered. "Well, not *his* daughter." Lucifer pointed to his body, and then snapped his fingers. "My daughter," he said—and it wasn't the devil in front of us anymore, but Loki.

CHAPTER NINETEEN

I DIDN'T EVEN REPLY TO SUCH AN ABSURD STATEMENT. I just stood there looking at the mischievous god, waiting for him to change back into Lucifer, or to say, "Gotcha!"

Raphael looked puzzled, but less indignant than me. "What do you mean?" he asked.

Loki grinned and walked up to me. "You are my daughter, Hel."

"How could that possibly be? My mother died before I could even be born, and my father committed suicide on her grave," I scoffed.

"Everything in your past—everything—was to prepare you to fulfill your destiny," Loki said. He motioned for all of us to go sit by the fire. "Come on, I will tell you the story."

Loki undid the ropes on Raphael's hands, then sat in the lone chair. Raphael and I sat at his feet on the rug, like anxious children.

"When my father found out I was having a child with Angrboda, your mother, he didn't want you in Asgard. Your mother was the known as the grief bringer, and Odin believed no good could come of you being born in our land, but said he would allow you to rule in the underworld. *You* would be the one to determine the destination of the souls that belong to our people. So when it was time for you to be born, we had you in the above world. You had to be born in blood and death—you had to know pain and loss as well as you knew breathing. You had to understand death, and heartbreak, and know the pain of dying in a mortal body. It was the only way." He paused, and looked at me with eyes that managed to be compassionate, yet cold. "Now, all of this," he looked around the room, "was not in the plan. When Persephone turned the palace over to you, you were supposed to step into your role as Queen of the Underworld. But Hades hadn't agreed to the situation, and decided to put his meddling ass in the game. When I heard Lucifer was stepping in, I knew you would need some help from dear old Dad," he winked.

Too many things were running through my mind, at too fast a speed for any of them to come out of my mouth. I barely noticed Raphael's hand on my shoulder, trying to comfort me.

Loki watched me closely for a minute or so, and then stood up, nearly jumping out of the chair. "Well, if you don't have anything to say, we really should be going before they figure out I'm not their 'dark prince,' shouldn't we?"

He led the way through one of the doorways, and into another nearly-hidden room, not even as large as a small closet. I saw a ladder leading up beyond the range of any normal person's vision.

Loki said, "Start climbing," and was the first one up the ladder.

I followed second, and Raphael was behind me. I had only made it up a few rungs before realizing the ladder was made from human bones. I cringed, and tried not to think too much about it as I wrapped my hand around what I assumed was a femur. I had enough to process at the moment.

The higher we climbed, the more my arms started to shake. I could feel Raphael behind me, and just barely make out Loki in front of me; but it was so dark I couldn't see anything close around me.

Of course, the thought of falling entered my mind: slipping and tumbling back down all that way—back into the den of the devil—and very likely taking Raphael with me when I fell. I was very careful as I climbed.

"Doing ok, baby?" Raphael asked after a time.

"Yeah," I said, with more confidence than I felt. "How are you doing?"

"I'm fine," he said.

"Aren't the two of you just adorable," Loki called from above us.

The ladder suddenly shook more violently than it had the whole time the three of us were climbing. We stopped moving and waited. It shook again, and again.

"Well, that isn't good," Loki said. "We need to move considerably faster."

"What is it?" I asked.

"They're coming after us," he said.

"Shit," I swore under my breath. It wasn't bad

enough to be climbing this creepy, unstable ladder, in the dark—now demons were climbing up after us.

We all climbed faster, not sure how quickly the demons could gain on us.

"Not much farther," Loki said, and I hoped he was right.

I heard a grunt, and a thud, followed by a long scream that ended before it seemed like the sound was finished.

I swallowed hard and fought the urge to stop climbing, knowing we couldn't spare the time.

"Raphael?" I asked softly.

"I'm OK. One of the bastards grabbed my foot, and I kicked him in the face," he said, and I heard the uneasiness in his voice.

"One down!" Loki cheered.

I giggled, half in amusement, half in horror.

The darkness became thicker the higher we climbed, and the air was cooler, which made no sense, since we were going up. I could no longer even make out the shadows cast by Loki, and I was afraid of us running into each other as we climbed.

"Stop," Loki said. "We're here, I just have to figure out how to open the gate from this side."

Raphael and I stopped climbing as we listened to him mumbling and struggling in the darkness.

After a few long moments, with the ladder still shaking as the bad guys continued to come after us, Raphael asked, "Is there anything we can do to speed this up?"

"I need someone's blood," Loki said, and sighed. "The gate in the tunnels is opened by fire, and this one is opened by blood."

Raphael immediately volunteered. "Do you have something sharp?"

"I got this," I said, ripping the bandage off of my wrist with my teeth. The wound had scabbed over, but would bleed easily enough if scratched.

I held my arm up to Loki; I couldn't scrape off the scab *and* keep my balance on the ladder. Besides, I was already getting lightheaded knowing I would be bleeding in a moment.

I felt Loki messing with my wrist, and steadied myself. Thankfully, after a moment, and not much pain, he said, "Got it," and gave me my arm back.

Suddenly, above us, there was light. My heart jumped with excitement, and I urged Loki to hurry up.

We climbed out of the hole, and I collapsed onto the black brick street, while Loki sealed the gateway with another few drops of my blood. I didn't even care this time.

The world spun around me, and I closed my eyes like I might fall off. My body started to tremble, and I was suddenly sweating and freezing at the same time. *Is this shock?* I felt a hand grip mine, and knew it was Raphael.

Just the feeling of his hand in mine calmed me; I opened my eyes, and there he was. He was stretched out beside me on the street, black hair spread out like a fan, his pale skin lovely and perfect against the ebony brick. I smiled and let out the breath I was holding. I'd done it: I'd gone to Hell, and brought him home.

CHAPTER TWENTY

We heard the demons trying to get through the gateway, and backed away.

"It'll hold for a while. That gateway shouldn't even be here. Hades needs to seal it permanently," said Loki, seeming rather casual about the subject.

Once my mind had a moment to calm down, I realized we were in the Vampire Quarter down one of the alleyways. I guess if you were going to hide a portal to Hell somewhere in the underworld, this was the right place.

"So Lucifer has just been able to come and go as he pleases here, for who knows how long?" I asked.

Loki shrugged, "Yes, but he really doesn't enjoy leaving Hell, so I don't think he's used it frequently."

The thought still didn't settle well with me. "Now what do we do?"

Loki smiled. "First, we need to get you back to Hades and ask him to close the doors. Second, we need to secure your position in rulership. Third, I need to go home."

We followed him through the Quarter and back into the city.

"What if I don't want to rule? I don't want to determine where souls go, that's what the soul contracts are for!" I protested.

"It's your destiny, Hel. Don't fight stepping into your power," he said without even turning around.

I still watched him with suspicion. *How can I be his daughter?* He looked so young himself.

"What power? I've never had the power to do anything!" I heard my voice getting louder as I got more upset.

He turned back to me and smiled. "More power than you can dream of."

Raphael was silent, but kept my hand in his as we rounded the next street and approached the white palace.

Loki didn't even bother knocking, just opened the door and went inside.

Two guards just inside the garden area eyed us suspiciously, but didn't stop us from entering.

I watched as Raphael tried to take in all of the magnificence, as we hurriedly walked through the lush greenery and past the little pond. I had forgotten how beautiful and overwhelming it was on first glance. I hated that we couldn't stop so that he could enjoy it.

"Hades!" Loki shouted, as we searched room to room. "We need to have a meeting at once."

I saw the faintest blur against one of the walls, and moved more closely. "Are you one of Melinoe's guards for the day?" I asked the spirit.

"I am," said a voice much deeper than I anticipated out of something barely there.

I jumped, but regained my composure. "Could you

get her for us, please?

The spirit moved away from the wall and into a nearby room.

Moments later, the ghost was back against the wall, and Melinoe was coming out of her room, trying to fix her hair with her fingers, and adjusting her shirt. Her eyes got big when she saw us.

"I can't fucking believe it! You made it back." She truly sounded astonished. She walked over and clapped me on the shoulder, like a guy would generally do.

She hit me on my injured arm and I gasped, clutching my arm to my chest.

"Ooh, sorry," she said, glancing at my arm. "Well, no one would have believed you survived Hell if you didn't have a few battle scars."

I was just about to say something to her when she walked past me and introduced herself to Raphael.

"You must be the great love that Hel was so determined to save. I'm not terribly fond of men, but I must say I can understand the appeal," she said, putting a black finger to her lips and looking him up and down.

Raphael gave her his best smile and pulled me in close to him, kissing me on the head. "Hel's pretty amazing for being my heroic rescuer. And who are you?"

Melinoe's lips quirked in amusement, realizing he wasn't falling for her flirty games. "I am Melinoe," she said, "daughter of Hades."

"Is he around?" I cut in.

She turned her attention back to me. "In the tunnels, I believe, searching for Cerberus."

I covered my mouth, remembering I had told the dog to wait for me at the entrance to Hell. I hoped he was OK.

"Can we go find him?" I asked.

"Rest. I'll have someone bring you some food, and tea. My guards and I will find them," she assured me.

The three of us sat down in the main living area and tried to relax, even if it was just for a moment. Melinoe took charge, making sure we were looked after, and we were all grateful for the sandwiches and drinks that were brought to us.

The sound of someone yawning loudly made me look over my shoulder, back towards Melinoe's room. Grace was standing in the doorway, rubbing her face and putting her eye patch in place.

"Mel," she said, "I thought you were coming back to bed."

"Grace?" I made her name a question—not the *Is it really you?* kind of question, but more in the, *That had better not be you,* way.

"Hel!" Grace screamed, and ran to me. "Oh my god, Hel, you're back! Does Ray know? Does Soren?" she rambled.

I shook my head no, and gave her my most stern glare. "What the fuck, Grace?" My hands were on my hips, and I had no intention of talking about myself right now.

"You don't get to scold me, Hel." Grace almost yelled it at me, but fought to keep her tone neutral. "You are the one who took off without even telling us your plan. We were sure we'd never see you again. You tossed all of us aside to traipse around after some guy who you knew for a few *weeks* before you died.

Don't act like you care that much about what, or who, I do."

Ouch. "I'm sorry, Grace. Of course I care. I just worry, and I didn't want to see things get bad between you and Boude. He really loves you," I said, taking her hand in mine.

Grace sighed, and wasn't happy the argument was ending that easily. "Yeah, well Sor.."

"Meet Raphael!" I urged a bit too enthusiastically as I cut her off.

Introducing Raphael to my friends felt strange. When he had been in my life, I hadn't had anyone else important. Now I had several friends who all knew about him, but I hadn't had time to tell him much of anything about them.

All the anger in Grace's face vanished as she grabbed Raphael and hugged him. "She missed you so much," Grace told him.

This was getting embarrassing.

Grace, Raphael, and I all ate and chatted as we awaited Melinoe's return with Hades and the big doggy. Loki excused himself for a nap.

I was starting to feel slightly less freaked out, and more distant from all of the events that had recently transpired, as we sipped our tea, and even laughed a time or two.

Grace was captivated with the story of how I got to Hell, and how Raphael and I found each other.

"That's just the most brilliant love story," she cooed.

"Umm, no. No, Grace, it was terrifying, and we

wouldn't have even made it out if it hadn't been for Loki," I explained, finally saying out loud that Loki was apparently my father.

"You're a goddess," Grace said quietly, and took a drink of her tea, leaving a red lipstick print on the white cup. "You're a motherfucking goddess!" She stood up and leaned across the table towards me.

I instinctively leaned back and looked at Raphael, who let out the chuckle he'd been trying repress.

"I can't wait to tell Andreas," Grace said smugly, and plopped back down in her chair.

That made me laugh; he was going to be so pissed.

"Is everyone still at the mansion?" I asked.

"Yes. Well, Andreas's shop is open again—all of the businesses are," Grace said.

I tried not to look directly at her when I asked the next questions. "How long was I gone, and does Boude know about Melinoe?"

"Long enough for all of us to believe you weren't coming back, and no," she answered.

"Maybe that's a discussion you should go have before things get more complicated," I suggested.

"You're right, I know," she whined. "I just came here to help her search the tunnels for you, and then things happened."

I laughed. "You and your rescue missions. I appreciate the effort, I guess. That is, if you ever did search for me."

Grace looked offended. "Of course we searched for you, but she told me it was no use."

"Go back to the mansion and tell everyone I'm back—you can tell them everything. Tell them about Hell, Raphael, and even Loki. It will save me time when I get there. Talk to Boude. I'll be there as soon as I can," I told her.

Grace stood up from her chair, resigned to handle all the drama I had just asked her to. "OK." She stepped around the table and hugged me. "Hurry back to us." She hugged Raphael again and headed towards the door. "Oh, and let Mel know I'll be back when I can."

"I will," I told her.

I looked at Raphael and took his hand again. I still couldn't believe he was here.

"What are you thinking?" he asked.

"Just how happy I am," I told him.

"For real? You're still happy in all of this mess?" His eyes held disbelief.

"Yep, as long as I get to keep you," I smiled.

He leaned in and kissed me, filling my stomach with butterflies that seemed to flutter all the way up to my chest. "For as long as you want."

CHAPTER TWENTY-ONE

A HIGH PITCHED WHINE, FOLLOWED BY DEEP rumbling bark, was my first hint that everyone was back. I barely had time to look over my shoulder before I was knocked backwards onto the floor by two huge paws. No matter which direction I turned my head, I couldn't escape the slobbery kisses of one, or all three, heads.

"Cerberus!" I laughed, as I tried to push him off. I finally gave into his excitement, and wrapped my arms around his back to hide my face against his body. At least that way I didn't risk drowning in drool.

It took both Hades and Raphael to pull the dog off of me. I stood up, attempting to smooth out my hair, and then used the tail of my shirt to dry my face. *So sweet, so gross.*

Hades shook his head, looking at the dog. "Traitor," he huffed.

Cerberus leaned against my side, tail thumping happily on the floor.

"Was he still waiting for me in the tunnels?" I asked.

"Right over the entrance," Hades said.

I rubbed the head in the center. "Such a good boy."

Melinoe had taken the chair Grace was in before, and was kicked back with her legs propped on the table, her feet hanging off the edge, as if to say she wasn't a total heathen.

Raphael was at my side petting Cerberus, and I saw Hades looking him up and down.

"Hades, this is Raphael. Raphael, meet Hades," I introduced.

"Pleasure," Raphael said, giving the god of the underworld a deep bow of his head.

Hades smirked, and gave Raphael a long lingering stare, being sure to meet the other man's eyes.

Raphael flinched when he realized he was seeing his own reflection in Hades's mirrored eyes. I couldn't blame him; it was very disconcerting.

Hades didn't actually respond to the introduction, but didn't seem like he was trying to be intentionally rude either. He just motioned for us all to take a seat, and sent one of Melinoe's guards to fetch Loki so that we could all talk.

Loki came into the room a few minutes later, yawning and stretching. "Pardon me, I only nap every few years or so. It takes me a while to wake up."

Hades rolled his eyes at the other god, and said, "Shall we discuss everything that's happened? I admit, I'm not very certain of where things stand, since I didn't expect you to make it back." The last words were directed at me.

"I don't think you counted on my father helping me," I grinned.

Hades glanced back at Loki. "Yes, well, there was some debate over whether or not there was any truth to that rumor."

Loki bit into a bright green apple, and with his mouth still full said, "Now, you know there is."

"So now what?" I asked. "What of your little contest, and the souls? When are you going to seal the gateways again? What happens after that?"

Hades looked down at the table where his hands were resting. "Those are the questions on my mind as well. I hadn't expected things to get quite this complicated."

"And that is precisely why you should have held the agreement in place, instead of getting your feelings hurt and doing things your own way," a new voice said as she entered the room.

We all stood, Hades included, and watched as Persephone came to the table. She first walked up to Hades and smiled at him. He hesitated to move forward, obviously nervous about the wrath he was likely to receive, and deserved.

She leaned in and kissed her dark husband. "What am I going to do with you?" she asked playfully. Relief washed over Hades's face, and he looked at her with big puppy-dog eyes. "I can't believe you tried to lock me out of my own kingdom." She shook her head. "As if I don't have my own secret doors."

"Hello, mum," Melinoe said, coming over to give her mother a hug.

"Hello. You've played both sides of this, I'm guessing?" Persephone asked her daughter.

Melinoe smirked, "Well, I mean, I have to listen to both of you, right? Might as well use your quarrels to my advantage. Oh and by the way, Dad tried to have his way with Hel, and had her entombed when she wouldn't agree."

Persephone closed her eyes and let out a long breath. She motioned for her daughter to step away so she could talk to us, after giving Hades a nasty look.

The Queen turned to me. "Hel, I am so sorry that your inauguration into the royal life has been such a dreadful one. I had hoped it would be peaceful for you." She turned to glare at Hades again. He looked away.

Trying to think of what to say, I finally settled on, "I appreciate you trying to help me step into my power, but I don't want to be a ruler."

Loki sighed, like he was tired of explaining it to me already. "It is your destiny."

I let him see how annoyed I was. "To Hell with destiny. I want to make my own way and choose things for myself from now on!"

The gods in the room with me looked absolutely baffled and appalled. Persephone looked sympathetic, like a mother explaining to her child that they had to go to school, or that she couldn't bring the family pet back to life.

"If you find a way to beat destiny, I will bow down before you. Many have tried, and running works for a while, but it always catches up with you. It is far better to embrace what the stars have aligned, and try to find a way to satisfy our hearts desires while doing what we are meant to do." Her voice held the knowledge of ancient lifetimes.

I knew she was right, but I didn't have to like it. I crossed my arms and looked away from everyone, trying to keep the first of the angry tears from escaping my eyes.

Instead of moving in to comfort me, Raphael stepped

slightly in front of me, to block everyone's view while I composed myself—another reason to love him.

"Queen Persephone, where should we start with the situation we are in right now?" Raphael asked.

"That is something for us to decide after a long discussion." She turned to Hades. "Please summon Lucifer. All of us need to reach an agreement."

"Do I need to stay?" I asked.

"No, go back to wherever your friends are. The underworld is in no condition for you to run right now. Let us get things settled, then we'll talk about things with you. Go. Rest, and enjoy those you love," she said sweetly.

"Thank you," I said, and left with Raphael by my side.

"You've been quiet through all of this," I said to Raphael as we walked.

"I don't know anything about this part of the underworld. I couldn't begin to give you advice," he said.

"Do you think I'm crazy for not wanting to fulfill my destiny?"

"No, not if it would make you unhappy."

"Deciding the fates of souls would not make me happy," I said.

"What would? I mean, if you could do anything you wanted, what would you choose?"

It surprised me that I had to think so hard to answer him. All I had wanted for so long was just to have him back with me. *I got him, so now what do I want.*

"If I could have anything that I wanted, I would go back with you to my cabin, my cemetery, and we would still take that beach trip together, and forget all of this." I shook my head at the ridiculousness of it. "But I would settle for us living and working here, as long as we were happy."

"You would want to continue being a reaper?" he asked.

I shrugged. "Yeah, I enjoy it. What would make you happy?"

He shook his head, and his eyes had lost some of their magic. "I have no idea," he answered.

I had to admit that it hurt my heart for him not to say something along the lines of, "I'll be happy as long as I'm with you," or some other kind of sappy reply. I knew his time in Hell was haunting him. I was there practically no time at all, and I knew it would always haunt me. I just wished that I knew how to help him.

CHAPTER TWENTY-TWO

I ENTERED THE MANSION TO THE ANGRY FACES OF most of my friends. Maybe letting Grace come ahead and tell them everything had been a bad idea. Instead of being relieved to see me and hearing about what happened, they had had time to sit and dwell on all the worry I had caused them.

I understood, I really did. What I had done was selfish, as far as their feelings were concerned. But I didn't regret it—not at all.

They were plenty nice enough to Raphael when I introduced him, but even Ray would barely talk to me. Grace and Boude were nowhere to be seen, and I thought it best not to interrupt them.

Just so I knew that everyone was caught up, I explained we were waiting on the gods to have their meeting, and after that we would have some clarity. Ray nodded, and Billy sighed.

"I'm sorry," I said, "to all of you. I know you think what I did was reckless—and selfish—and I apologize if it made any of you feel like you weren't important to me. If you know me at all, though, you know I would've done the same thing for any of you."

Everyone watched, waiting for me to say more, but that was all I had. I was tired and hurt, and didn't have a clue what was going to happen next. I wanted some peace.

I turned away from everyone and went up the stairs to the room I had been staying in, listening for the sound of Raphael's footsteps behind me—but he didn't follow me.

I went inside the room, and was surprised to find Boude sitting on my bed. His head was in his hands, with his bright red hair draped around him.

He was surprised to see me as well. "Sorry, it was rude of me to use your room. I just needed a minute away without having to walk past everyone." He started to get up.

I held up my palm to stop him, and walked over to the bed to sit down next to him. "I'm sorry," I told him.

"Eternity," he sighed. "Sometimes it is daunting to face an eternity of love and heartache."

I rubbed his back gently. "Is that why most vampires become so emotionless?"

He nodded. "It takes practice, but feelings are something you can learn to live without."

"When the two of you got together, I could only think about you hurting her, and how sad I would be for my friend. It never dawned on me that she could hurt you, and I that I would still be so sad for my friend." I squeezed his shoulder.

Boude patted my leg beside him. "Thank you, Helena." He dried his damp eyes, and straightened himself into the classy posture I was so used to seeing from him. "Enough sadness; we still have reason to celebrate. You survive Hell and saved your true love!" he cheered.

I gave him a half-hearted smile. "And everyone downstairs hates me because they think I'm a selfish bitch." My voice was cheerful and loaded with sarcasm.

"You would've done the same if it had been any of us. That's hardly selfish," said Boude.

"That's what I said!"

The door was cracked, but Raphael still knocked before peeking inside. "May I come in?" he asked.

"Sure," I told him.

Boude stood up and straightened himself out as Raphael came into the room.

"Boude, this is Raphael; Raphael, meet Boude," I introduced.

The man and vampire shook hands.

"I need to be going," said Boude. "Thank you for chatting with me, and congrats on your success."

"Anytime," I replied as I watched him leave.

He made sure to pull the door closed until the latch clicked.

Raphael stood in front of me, looking down to meet my eyes. "Everything OK?"

"Eh, he and Grace are…" I started.

"Ohh, that's Grace's boyfriend, who I'm guessing is now her ex." Raphael put the pieces together.

"Yeah," I said, and laid back on the bed.

Raphael climbed on top of me, straddling me and looking down at my face. "I think you could use an orgasm," he said, and I watched the most delightful grin spread across his face.

I laughed, and felt the warmth of it spread up my

face and down the rest of my body. "I think that's an excellent observation."

He kissed me deeply as his hands first explored my body over the clothes I had on, then slipped under my shirt.

"We still haven't showered," I breathed.

"Shhh." Raphael silenced me with his tongue in my mouth again.

Once undressed, he was back on top of me, his fingers sliding in and out of me to make sure I was ready for him.

Once he was satisfied with how wet he had gotten me, he took my wrists in his hands and asked, "Does it still hurt?" inclining his head towards the injury.

I shook my head no, but said, "Just be easy."

Raphael put my arms overhead and pinned me to the bed. My hips arched up to his, wanting to feel him inside me. He kissed me for a long time, letting that desire build and build; but the longer he waited, the more desperate I felt, and my attention turned from lust to fear.

I was pinned, helpless in his grip, and moving my arms meant potentially hurting myself. I couldn't even turn my head away from his aggressive kiss to tell him to stop or catch my breath. My vision went fuzzy and dark, and when I tried to focus on Raphael, instead I saw the other demons we had seen in Hell—not the sexy ones, the scary ones—beings that looked half decomposed, with bits of raw flesh hanging from the red muscle and glistening bone underneath. In my mind's eye, they smiled at me, happy they were still able to hurt me, maybe in the worst way possible: by ruining sex with the man that I loved in a place that

I was supposed to feel safe. The smell of sulfur and decay filled my nostrils, and my mouth filled with saliva, like it does before you're going to be sick.

I forced my eyes to look around the room, for something, anything else to focus on. To my horror, as my eyes scanned any open spaces, there were more creatures looking back at me.

Meanwhile, Raphael didn't even notice that I was enduring this torment, and seemed to be totally unaffected. He was kissing me like everything was perfectly fine, like I was just as into him as I was when we started. *How is he not feeling this? I'm not turned on anymore, I'm terrified. I have to get away.*

I wiggled and pushed against him, and gave a small but firm kick to his leg that made him pull back and release my hands. The moment I was free I pushed away from him and got off of the bed. "I can't breathe," I said.

Raphael's face was panic stricken. "What's wrong, what can I do?" he asked.

I shook my head and sat on the floor underneath the window. *How am I going to tell him without making him feel terrible about himself?* It was so awful, and so bizarre that I couldn't begin to explain it. It was downright embarrassing now, looking around the room and everything being perfectly normal. Raphael loved me—was waiting for me in my bed—and I was afraid to go to him.

"Hel, you have to talk to me. What happened?" Raphael came to sit beside me and put his hand on my shoulder. It took every ounce of strength I had not to pull away in revulsion.

"I don't know. It was like a nightmare. I knew it was

you, but I kept seeing all of these awful things, and I couldn't move, or tell you. I know it wasn't real but…" I closed my eyes and felt the first tears fall.

"You saw scary things while I was on top of you?"

I nodded and looked away, choking back the urge to ugly-cry. "Imagine the thing from your worst nightmare was having sex with you, and it felt as real as you sitting here with me."

Raphael's face went blank as he tried to process my words. With nothing to say, he moved in closer and wrapped his arms around me. My stomach lurched, and I gagged as I moved out of his embrace.

I loved Raphael, and the fact that I'd almost thrown up because he tried to comfort me? Well, now I felt like the worst person ever.

I held it in while I got dressed, thankful to have a change of clothes here even if I wasn't clean. I didn't turn back once to look at Raphael. I still kept it together as I went down the steps and past Billy and Margaret on the couch.

"Running to the palace. Be back soon," I said without pausing.

The minute the mansion door shut behind me, I cried—I bawled. My eyes were so blurry I could barely see, and I used my shirt to wipe my runny nose more times than I wanted to count. As I passed others in the Quarter and through town, I didn't care if they saw my meltdown.

CHAPTER TWENTY-THREE

I WENT INTO THE PALACE, IGNORING THE GUARDS all together. I walked in and sat down on the smooth rocks surrounding the little pond. The sound of the rushing water from the ram's head helped calm the shaking breaths I was taking, and I picked a plum off of a nearby tree that was hanging within my reach, and bit into it.

It was the best thing I had ever tasted: so sweet and juicy, with just a touch of tartness from the peel. I closed my eyes and was savoring every bite.

"You look worse now than when you first came back from Hell," Melinoe said.

I opened my eyes and found her sitting near me on the rocks. She was picking up tiny pebbles between the larger stones and tossing them into the pond.

"Hell followed me back," I told her.

Her face went from intrigued to serious. She leaned in towards me, resting a tattooed elbow on her knee. "What do you mean—and don't be vague."

She said it with such intensity that I spilled the whole event: every feeling, everything I saw and smelled.

Melinoe listened intently, never interrupting. After

my story was over, she leaned back again and seemed to be thinking things over.

"Am I crazy? Did something follow us back from Hell? Is Raphael cursed?" More questions went through my mind, but those were the ones I asked aloud.

Melinoe stood up and reached over me to get a plum for herself, then sat back down. "Hel, do you remember me telling you that I'm a goddess of nightmares?"

My stomach suddenly seemed heavy. "I do," I answered. "You didn't have anything to do with this, though, right?"

She took a bite of the plum and shook her head. "I have no reason to cause you nightmares, and that can only be done when someone is in a suggestible state—asleep, or close to it. Demons haven't marked you or Raphael, and they haven't followed you back from Hell, or you wouldn't be sitting here," she said with utter certainty.

"They couldn't just be messing with me, from far away?" I asked.

"In the living world and the underworld, demons have to be close by to influence you. In the living world, they can shift their energy to be virtually invisible. They can't do that here—you'd know if there was a demon around you," she said.

"Raphael said he became a demon while he was in Hell. Maybe it's who he is now—something he can't escape."

"Nope, he is not a demon. True demons were never human. They can be servants to Lucifer, and sometimes are referred to as demons for the sake of convenience, but they aren't. Real demons are the only living creatures made without souls. Whatever detestable things Raphael might have done as a servant will play on his conscience, but he has no power to do what you described," Melinoe said.

"Then what does have that power, or who?" I asked.

Melinoe tried to hide the smile I saw by biting her lip. "Ironically, it was your soul."

"What?" I asked, not even angry, just confused.

"Yep, tricky bastards those souls," she laughed. "Your soul directs you towards your destiny. Every wish, desire, and need that you feel is your soul steering you in the direction you are meant to go in."

"But I don't want my destiny, at all! I have no *desire* to rule. Why would my soul lead me there? All I've wanted since the moment I met Raphael was to love and be with him." I felt like I was going in twisted circles.

Melinoe laughed again. "Helena, where has this obsession with Raphael led you? Every single thing you've done to be with him, to save him, to love him, has led you to this very point, to the edge of fulfilling what was meant for you. Your soul chased him because he was how you would get here."

"Fine, so I'm fucking here!" I yelled. "Why am I being tormented now for loving him after going through all of that?"

Her charming smile had faded, and there was a sternness in her dark eyes. "Because he got you here, and that's as far as he can bring you on this journey."

"You're telling me my soul won't allow me to be with him now—that it's going to make things so unbearable that I can't stay with the man I love?" I was so hurt and betrayed… by my destiny—by my own goddamn soul! I would've ripped it out myself with a rusty spoon if things worked that way.

"Afraid so," she said softly.

An idea came to mind: something I had sworn that I would never do. Ray had always warned me to "never say never," or you would most certainly be tested on it.

"Melinoe, what would happen to my destiny if I got rid of my soul—if I became a vampire?"

Her eyes widened and her lips parted just slightly as she thought about what to say. "I haven't the faintest idea what would happen. But if that's what you're thinking of trying, you have to let me watch."

"Fine," I said. "We need to hurry, though. No one else can know, or they'll try to talk me out of it."

"Do you want me to send for Raphael, to see if he wants to be turned too?" Melinoe asked.

I considered it, but ultimately decided against involving him. I didn't even know what my feelings were about him, and what was being forced upon me by fate.

"No, just us. Let's go now," I said.

I sat on the couch in Andreas's apartment. He walked in front of me, pacing back and forth, trying to process my line of reasoning for wanting to be turned. Melinoe stood quietly in the corner, looking cool, and slightly dangerous—as always.

"Helena, I'm not sure about this. This seems very sudden, and I don't think you know what you're asking. If I do this and you regret it, you'll hate me,"

Andreas said, looking more uncertain than I had ever seen him.

"I trust you Andreas, and I do know what I'm asking. I want my soul to be gone. It's leading me towards a future that I don't want. I don't know if I love Raphael, or if it was all just tricks. I'll never be able to trust any feeling I have until it's gone. And if I do end up regretting it, I won't hate you—I promise," I reassured him.

"If you do this, your options are gone: no reincarnation, no chance at heaven, or anywhere but here. You *have* to have living blood, from breathing people, regularly… even if you find it disgusting." I saw him trying to think of all the other issues I might want to take into consideration.

"I know all of this. I was the one telling it to Grace before she turned," I told him, then smacked myself in the head. "Grace! She will hate me if she isn't here. Is she at the boutique?"

"She is," Andreas said.

"Melinoe, please go get her and bring her back here. Tell her I need her, but don't tell her what's going on until you get closer."

"On my way," she said. She pushed away from the wall, and walked out with her strong-yet-graceful androgynous walk. She was somehow both the bad girl and the bad boy we all crushed on in school.

After Melinoe was gone, Andreas remarked, "I do see what Grace sees in her."

"I know, right?" I agreed. I didn't have to approve of my friend's choice to understand it, but Boude was nothing to sneeze at, either.

While we waited for them to return, we talked a

little about Grace and Boude. I learned that Grace was back to staying here, and Boude would soon be back at his place, once all of Grace's things were out. I kept saying how much I hated that they split.

"Hel, nothing is permanent. It's fine to be sad about it, but you have to let it go. Grace might get her heart broken—that's OK. Boude is hurting now, but he'll recover."

"Do you think I'm making the right choice?" I asked him.

"It's not the choice I would make. If someone told me I was a god, and meant to be a judge of souls in the underworld, I'd put that crown on, and no being in eternity could make me give it up," he said, with a big smile. "However, I do understand wanting to be in total control of your decisions, and not having to wonder if something is influencing your every move."

We were quiet for a few minutes waiting for Mel and Grace to get back.

"Why haven't you asked me about Hell?" I asked Andreas. "Most people have been curious what it's like."

"I'm not. I don't need to know the specifics of suffering to know it exists. I like pleasure, and beautiful things. The ugly and unnecessarily painful don't interest me. If you need to talk to someone about the horrors you endured so that you don't have to carry it, I understand, but I'm not that person." His amber eyes were serious, and focused on mine.

I could find many flaws with Andreas and the way he chose to live, but his honesty wasn't one of them.

The door flew open and Grace came charging inside. "Are you really going to do it?" she squealed.

"I am," I smiled. "I hope you aren't mad that I asked Andreas instead of you."

"Oh Hell no. I don't want to be your maker," she laughed. "But I am happy you wanted me here. I was afraid you might still be angry over things with Boude and me."

"I love you both. Whether or not the two of you are in relationship together, that doesn't change," I told her.

"We really should get this show on the road," Melinoe called, once again back in the corner of the room where she could observe everything.

Grace squeezed my hand, and then went to help Andreas get everything set up on the floor, just like he had done when I watched him bring Grace over—only this time it would be me on the floor, laying in his arms as my soul died.

I admitted to myself that I was scared, but I wouldn't even consider backing out.

CHAPTER TWENTY-FOUR

Grace sat on the red couch with Melinoe. Grace's expression held almost as much excitement for me to turn as when she was brought over herself.

Melinoe was leaning forward, trying to make sure she could see every move.

I laid down on the soft furred throws and fluffy pillows that Andreas had prepared. He pulled the curtains closed, and lit a few candles before turning off the overhead light.

I raised an eyebrow at him and teased, "So what is it you're planning here?"

He winked at me and took off his shirt. Everything about Andreas was tan, golden, and warm. If he ever dressed casually, he would have fit right in with the California surfer guys. But with his love for fashion and luxury, that would never have truly suited him. "You remember this is an intimate experience," he said.

"I do," I replied. My heart thudded just a little too fast. I wondered if being held tight by Andreas while he drained my blood would trigger a similar reaction to one I had with Raphael during sex. I felt it was best to warn him. "Ugh, you know I told you about what happened in bed with Raphael. It shouldn't happen with you, but if it does, don't stop. Just get it over with."

"Hel, I don't want to do this if I have to hold you down," Andreas said, running a hand through his wavy hair.

"You won't have to hold me down," I told him, vowing to myself that if it happened, I'd just deal with it.

"Ready?" he asked.

I let out a deep breath. "Yes," I said, and I really was.

He knelt down facing me, and offered his hand for me to sit up.

I eyed his hand, having expected him to have leaned over me or laid down beside me to bite. After a moment I took it, and came up onto my knees.

Andreas stroked my hair and gently tucked it behind my ear. I closed my eyes and leaned in to him, bracing for the bite.

He leaned in close to me, but instead of biting, he whispered, "Hel, I've taken blood from you before. I made it as painless as I could then, but I can make it even better. Let me make this enjoyable for you." His hand against my lower back was firm, pulling me against his body.

Andreas had taken blood from me before. He had gone too long without feeding, and we had been captured. I gave him just enough to sustain him until he could hunt. My blood was dead, so it wasn't nourishing to him, but it kept him from getting weaker. Dead blood was kind of the vampire equivalent of junk food: it wasn't good for you, but it was better than dying. His bite hadn't been bad, and the feeling I'd had while he drank had been almost euphoric. *If that was without him even trying, how much better could it be?*

I was only going to do this once, so I said, "Make it good."

Andreas started tugging at my shirt to pull it off.

"Whoa, wait a second," I immediately protested.

"You're going to fight me on every step of this, aren't you?" Andreas sighed.

"I'm not having sex with you, and we have an audience," I reminded him.

"No sex, I swear, and I was only taking off your shirt to keep from getting blood on it—and skin to skin contact makes it more enjoyable. You can leave your bra on if that's more comfortable."

I expected to hear a giggle from Grace, but she was silent and focused on watching us.

I pulled my shirt off and tossed it to the side.

Andreas's warm fingers on my skin felt good, but I kept glancing at the two women on the couch.

Andreas whispered to me again. "Look into my eyes. It's just us. Forget there is anyone else in the world."

I looked up into his eyes that reminded me of jewels carved from amber, golden sunsets, and warm, sticky, delicious honey.

The longer I stared into those eyes, the more everything else melted away. I didn't see demons, but I saw myself. I watched as my body spiraled, and fell down through all that warmth and softness that Andreas's eyes and touch promised. I felt myself falling like Alice down the rabbit hole, but I wasn't afraid; it felt good. Distantly, I heard my name being called, but I was too far away.

I heard a voice whisper, "I'm going to kiss you now," and I leaned into it, even though I couldn't see the person in front of me.

With the sensation of the kiss, I felt the press of my body against another. *So warm, so safe.* It felt as though the other body was wrapped around me entirely, like there was someone holding me from behind, as well as someone in front of me. As the lips moved away from mine, I sank into the strong arms holding me from behind, but then there was softness again. I felt a sharp instant of pain that almost pulled me back into the moment, and my eyes fluttered open for only a second before sinking back into Wonderland. *How strange*, I thought, as this time I didn't spiral into a honey abyss, but floated up into night sky that glittered with emeralds instead of stars.

The last thing I heard was, "Drink," and as I swallowed, I tasted cinnamon and pennies.

My eyes opened and I couldn't see. It wasn't dark, so I knew that I wasn't blind, but I couldn't make out any of the colors or shapes that seemed like they were all pressed against my eyeballs.

"Hello?" I called out. I reached my hands out to my sides to get a feel for if I was still on the floor. I didn't want to roll off the couch if Andreas had moved me. I was trying not to panic about the whole not seeing issue. I felt slightly relieved when one hand touched the warm skin of a body laying next to me. When my hand touched another body on the other side… that's when I started getting nervous.

I shook the people on both sides of me. "Wake up. Wake up, wake up, wake up," I panicked.

Wanna know what's worse than waking up in bed with someone you didn't expect to, and not remembering the night before? Waking up with *two* people in bed with you, and not remembering the night before… Oh, and you can't see.

I heard a groan from the body on my left side. "Oh," he sighed with relief. "Thank goodness you're awake." It was Andreas.

"Why can't I see? It's like everything is so magnified it's blurry," I told him.

"Yes, vampires can essentially use their eyes to zoom in and out on things. Just imagine you're shrinking things down in your mind."

It took a couple of tries, but things went from huge blobs, to manageable, and finally to normal. "That is something I did not know," I said.

Once I could see, I didn't need to waste any time investigating the identity of the person on the other side of me. His long curls were tangled, and appeared to be the color of blood against his fair skin, in this dim lighting.

I moved a strand of hair from his face, and those green eyes opened. I recalled the last vision I'd had, of floating among the emerald stars. It had been Boude looking down at me.

He smiled and sat up, shirtless, the same as Andreas. I looked on either side of me and grinned to myself. Two beautiful men, half-naked, and tousle-haired, who had been holding me for hours, and I couldn't remember the details of it. *It fucking figures.*

"Before you freak out," Boude started, "none of us had sex."

I could see he was very concerned about me being upset with him. "We're all still wearing pants, so I figured we'd behaved, at least in that way."

"Yes," Andreas huffed. "We all behaved most respectably while you were floating about in the ethers. And I can't tell you how much I will forever regret not having had both you and Boude at the same time."

I touched his shoulder. "Thank you for being a gentleman."

He shrugged me off.

"I wouldn't say we were perfectly respectable," Boude said, as he put on his shirt and handed me mine. "There was a lot of touching and kissing, and tension."

My head was still a little foggy as I tried to think of things I needed to ask. "So where did Grace and Mel go? When did Boude get here? And who did I kiss?"

"You were unlike anyone I've ever brought over. I quickly saw I wasn't going to be able to handle you myself. Grace was starting to panic because your soul was trying to leave before I even bit you. I've never seen someone go under that quickly. She went to get Boude, but then she and Melinoe left so we could focus. It was a good thing she did, too. It took both of us to hold you and drain you. Not that you had more blood than an average person, but it was thick and rich. I couldn't have done it on my own. Then when I gave you blood, you wanted a lot more than I've ever had to give. Boude and I took turns sharing our blood with you. Oh, and you kissed us both," Andreas added.

I looked at the two men. "So both of you are my makers?"

"We are," Boude said.

"I didn't even know that was possible," I replied.

"It's not often done, but it's very possible," said Andreas.

I took one of their hands in each of mine. "Thank you. How can I ever repay you?"

Boude leaned in and kissed me on the cheek. "That's not how this works, love. No repayment needed."

"Well, that was a lot more work than most transitions. I was very concerned for your safety, and you know how I feel about stress. I think getting to have that threesome you got us so worked up for would be a fair repayment," Andreas suggested.

Boude and I had a good laugh about that.

CHAPTER TWENTY-FIVE

Andreas let me shower and put on some clean clothes that Grace had left there.

I stared at my eyes in the mirror. I had always been intrigued and mystified by vampire eyes. No white, no pupil, just faceted gems or swirling patterns that often looked like semi-precious stones. Now that I had my own, I still found them amazing.

Because Boude and Andreas had both assisted in turning me, my eyes weren't exactly like either of theirs. My eyes were chartreuse: a beautiful mix of golden honey and emerald green. When I turned my head in the light I caught little glimmers of flecks of gold and green, almost like glitter. I hadn't seen all the types of vampire eyes, but so far, mine were my favorite. My fangs were also new and fun to poke at, but not nearly as pretty.

"Stop admiring yourself and come on. You need to feed—now," Andreas urged.

I was not excited about this part, but it was a necessary evil that I was well aware of going into this. I followed the men back to the spot on the floor and laid back down between them.

"OK, so how do I do this?" I asked.

"Just close your eyes and let your mind drift away," Boude said. "We'll lead you through this to start."

I did as he said, and within a short amount of time, I was standing outside of a busy nightclub, on a street I'd never been on, in a city that I'd never visited. Of course it was nighttime, and with my new eyes, the colors of the neon lights were entrancing.

The air smelled like cotton candy, and suddenly my mouth was watering. "Where is that smell coming from?" I asked.

"What do you smell?" Andreas asked.

"Cotton candy." I could almost feel the texture of the fluffy spun sugar dissolving on my tongue.

"I smell steak," said Andreas.

"Roast pork," smiled Boude.

"Why are we all smelling different foods?" I asked.

Andreas said, "Actually, we are all smelling the same thing: blood. Our brains just interpret it as our favorite foods to make it more appealing."

"Wow, does that mean when I bite someone their blood will taste like cotton candy?"

"No," Boude replied. "It'll taste a million times better."

I had always thought it would be hard to make myself bite someone and drink their blood. I found it gross and inhuman, almost animalistic. After a while perusing the club and the occupants in the alley, I discovered that the part of me that thought those things was the human side of my brain.

My new vampire brain found the stalking and attack part of this very fun. Food was my reward: sweet, metallic blood that flowed into my mouth and down my throat—warm, and more filling than a five course meal.

We didn't kill anyone, and went back to our bodies sated, and a little drunk. I liked being a vampire.

"How do you feel about things now? What do you want to do, or what do you desire?" Andreas asked.

"I want to see Raphael, to see if those feelings are still there," I told him.

"What if he is repulsed by the fact that you turned?" Boude asked.

"Then it is what it is," I said calmly.

I made my way back to the mansion. I wanted to see Grace, but other things needed to be addressed first. Andreas had assured me he would let Grace know that I was doing well.

My decision was going to be tough for my friends to understand. I thought about Billy, and wondered if he would hate me now; Soren certainly would, if we ever saw one another again.

I dreaded opening the door, but knew I had to face everyone once again.

Raphael was sitting on the couch when I walked in. No one else was around. He didn't act surprised or repulsed as I walked closer. He was calm, and almost cold.

"Are you OK?" he asked; his tone was neutral.

"I am. I had to do this," I told him as I began to tell the story. I hadn't planned to dump all of it on him at once, but the words just poured out. I told him everything that had happened from the moment I ran out of the house, away from him, until now.

He nodded. "Well?"

"Well what?" I asked.

"Well, how do you feel about me now? Were all of the feelings we shared just your goddess destiny using me?" He sounded so angry. I really couldn't blame him.

"I didn't know that's what it was, Raphael. You know I would never have used you. You know I didn't want any part of being a goddess. I just gave up my soul so that I could get to the truth of this," I whined.

He put his hand on my leg. "You're right. I know you didn't know any differently. It's just a lot to process." He ran a hand through his long black hair. "And now you're a vampire, and I don't know what that means for us either."

"Does it bother you that I turned? It's OK if it does bother you. I didn't do it believing it would fix everything," I explained.

Raphael looked me over carefully and gazed into my new eyes. "Those are pretty," he said. "But it's hard for me to believe it's still you in there."

"That's fair. I'm sure the fangs will take some getting used to, on both our parts," I laughed.

"Uh, yeah," he laughed. "So how will we know if this worked?" he asked.

"I guess we will need to see if we can have sex," I told him plainly.

He seemed to mull this over, and then said, "Well everyone is out right now."

We made it upstairs in record time, but once the bedroom door closed behind us we both froze, afraid to make the next move. Neither of us wanted a repeat of the previous event.

"Just kiss me," I told him, "and check in with me now and then—and don't be rough."

Raphael leaned in to kiss me, and I kissed him back. I insisted on my tongue being in his mouth instead of vice versa; that way I could break the kiss if needed, and he wouldn't cut himself on my fangs.

As we kissed and undressed, I tried to gauge my feelings for him, now versus in the beginning. He was still beautiful, he was still fun to kiss, and the things he did to my body felt good. But whatever it was that had captivated me so deeply and passionately, it wasn't there anymore.

I pushed the sadness away and enjoyed the time with him. He was still a good lover, and from his reactions to the things I did, my own skills had improved. I was grateful that I wasn't haunted by the faces of demons this time, but the ghost of our past was hanging overhead.

CHAPTER TWENTY-SIX

After sex, I stayed in bed with Raphael, trying to decide if I needed to tell him now and make an honest break, or wait until I knew how things were going at the palace.

"Where is everyone?" I asked.

Raphael answered, "Your old boss came by and said Billy could come back to work, that people were dying again. So Margaret was going back to work, and Ray decided to go too, and see if he could get assigned."

My heart jumped at his words. "Soren, came by? He was in the Quarter?" I didn't hide my shock.

"Yeah, I guess he needed Billy's help. He asked if you were coming back, but none of us could tell him anything, since we didn't know where you were."

I knew that Soren would have dug up every single body himself before coming into the Quarter. Something was wrong.

I didn't want to be too obvious, so I stretched and yawned and said, "Well, I should probably go get caught up on everything, and let Hades and Persephone know I won't be ruling."

"Do you want me to come with you?" Raphael

asked, still naked and cozy in the bed.

"You should probably see about getting assigned as well, or at least catch up with Ray. It sounds like things are getting back to normal," I suggested.

"OK, I'll do that. Should we plan for all of us to meet back here later?" he asked.

"That sounds good," I said, feeling a bit absent minded as I hurried to get dressed.

He sat up and leaned towards me, obviously waiting for a kiss goodbye. Since I wasn't ready to have *the* discussion about us just yet, I met his reach and gave him the quickest of kisses before skipping down the stairs.

I was getting really tired of trekking back and forth between the Vampire Quarter and the rest of the underworld. I wondered where I would finally settle once everything else was decided. I still couldn't imagine myself living in this place. It was beautiful, gothic, and intricate, with lovely designs and menacing sharp edges everywhere you looked. I could fully appreciate the planning that had gone into the architecture now, with my super-vision; but it was still dark, and I still didn't really care for vampires outside of my close circle. *Am I allowed to be a vampire living out of the Quarter?* I wondered.

I came to the street in town where I needed to decide if I was going to the palace first, or going to the fields. I knew going to the fields would be pointless if I didn't first go the palace and make sure my new condition had canceled out my destiny. Right it was.

So many locations I could be visiting in the underworld, and yet it seemed I was always in the same few places.

Loki greeted me at the door; his face wasn't young and cheerful looking anymore. "What have you done?" his voice rumbled several octaves deeper than I had heard come out of him.

"You, all of you," I said, flinging my hand at the whole of the palace, "forced me to do this so that I could make my own choices."

His eyes were so full of anger. "You do not know what you've done," he said through gritted teeth and walked away from me.

I expected my welcome from Hades and Persephone would be about as warm, but I needed to know what the plan was, and who was in charge now.

I walked into the garden and saw Persephone standing nearby, having just watched my argument with my father. She was so still I hadn't immediately noticed her.

"Do you feel the same way?" I asked, when she saw me looking at her.

She shook her head. "Don't you think I would have done the same to have avoided my own destiny? Don't you think Loki, the God of Mischief, would have done that—or much worse—to get out of much less?" she laughed.

"So I did it? By getting rid of my soul, do I now get to decide my own destiny?" I asked.

"I can't say that I believe it is all that easy, but for now at least, yes," she admitted, and gave a deep and elegant curtsy.

I remembered her earlier promise. Having the queen of all of the underworld curtsy to me didn't make me feel like I had won, though. I laughed awkwardly and motioned for her to stand.

"So now what? Who is ruling? Are the gates closed?" I asked.

"The gates are indeed closed, and Lucifer's little hidden passageway has been sealed. The souls that made it here from Hell are being screened to see if they can in fact stay. Lucifer is angry that he wasn't able to convince any more souls to follow him back to Hell." She giggled and it lit up her face.

"He seemed charming enough, but I guess he just wasn't that good a trickster after all," I mused.

"He's a brilliant trickster, but Loki is better. Up against anyone else, Lucifer would have cleaned up with souls, who would have happily followed him back to the pit. The souls Loki won have already gone to their new places, and the door was closed. Loki is just here until things with you are done."

"Guess I killed his dream of a perfect family," I scoffed.

"My dear, if you can show me one perfect family in the history of gods and goddesses, I'll be impressed. He will get over it," she said. "So since you aren't taking over the underworld, I will continue to oversee things, and it will run as it always has. What are your plans for yourself now that you are free to choose your own way?"

I felt immense relief knowing that Persephone would still be in charge. She was the only one of these crazy deities that I even remotely trusted not to let things go up in flames. At the very least, I believed she wouldn't set the fire.

"I'm not sure. I don't think I want to live in the Vampire Quarter, and I would love to go back to reaping, but I'm not sure there's still a place for me there. So much has changed," I sighed.

"Will your Raphael come with you?" Persephone asked, with curiosity sparkling in her brown eyes. As spring faded in the living world, her hair and eyes were returning to their darker shades.

"I don't think so. He doesn't feel like mine anymore," I told her.

"I see. That's OK; paths cross, destinies unfold, and then everything gets shaken up so that it can start all over again. In time, love will find you again," she smoothed my hair and gave me a sweet smile. "Go see if there is still a place for you in the fields," she said.

"What about Loki. Do I need to make some kind of amends?" I asked.

She shook her head. "Families of gods do not make amends in that way. In time, he will forget, and he might contact you again." She shrugged, "Or he might not, and either way, you will be fine."

I waved to her and left the palace, hoping that I wouldn't be returning anytime soon.

My stomach felt like a big tangled mess as I approached the fields. I felt like the prodigal son (or would it be daughter?), returning home and hoping I would be accepted.

Soren had been very clear on his opinions of vampires from the first time I had met him. After getting to know Boude and Grace a little better, he had admitted that maybe they weren't all bad. However, he had shared my belief that a soul was far too valuable a thing to give up, even to be a vampire. I had believed that too, until I learned that wasn't always the case.

Soren might not even be there, or might not even speak to me, if Eira was still making decisions for him.

I recalled our last conversation at the shed before I left for Hell, and his confession. I wasn't certain I was ready for that conversation either, but it was better than the one I needed to have with Raphael.

Out in the distance I saw the silhouettes of Billy and Soren digging. I wanted to run to them and throw myself into their arms, then grab my own shovel and jump in beside them.

I didn't run, though; I kept a steady pace, and hoped that they would still love me—that they would still be my friends.

"Hey guys," I said when I got a little closer.

"Hel!" Billy said, and he actually sounded excited to see me; he hadn't noticed yet.

"What you doing here, your highness?" Soren asked, looking all huge and serious.

I remembered how he intimidated me when I was first around him. Now I just smiled. "That royal life wasn't for me. Give me a blue-collar job any day," I said.

I saw the hint of smile at the corner of his mouth. He moved toward me. "Welcome back," he said. I knew he saw my eyes, because as he said "back," his voice dropped and the touch of his smile was gone.

I held my breath as I waited for him to say something else, but he didn't. There was a soft grunting noise as he looked me over, but he said nothing about my change. He did ask, "Are you really back?"

I swallowed. "If you'll have me."

He narrowed his eyes at me and was quiet. Billy

walked in closer now, and he didn't hide his surprise when he saw my eyes.

"Holy shit, Hel! You turned? You're a vampire now?" He was inches from my face, inspecting me like a strange bug.

"I had a good reason," I told him.

"Do you want your old house back?" Soren ignored all of the vampire talk.

"If it's available."

"Of course, I just thought you might need something bigger if you weren't coming alone," he said. Such a subtle way to ask a tricky question.

"I'm coming alone," I said. *Dammit*, I didn't have a good way to ask him if Eira was still around—unless I decided to be obvious.

"How is Eira?" I asked. I decided I was OK with obvious.

Billy grinned and made a whistling sound as he walked away from the two of us, giving us the illusion of privacy.

Soren turned a little red and looked away for a moment. "Eira is gone. She decided to follow Loki and spend her afterlife away from me. We remembered our life together very differently. I couldn't keep apologizing for things I didn't remember doing, and she couldn't forgive me. And by the same token, she wasn't the woman I remembered either. I'm not sure where we lost each other, but it was irreparable," he said.

"I'm sorry," I said, and meant it. "You didn't want to choose another afterlife?"

"After all this time?" he laughed. "No, this is my eternity: this is home for me. Where is your Raphael?"

I was getting really tired of hearing him called that. "We weren't the same people as before either," I said, and left it at that, for now.

"I'm sorry," he said, but I don't think he meant the words as much as I had.

I continued with my bluntness. "Where does this leave us? Am I back to just working under you, or is there more?"

"What do you want?" he asked.

I watched his hand flex around the handle of his shovel, and saw the muscles tense all through his upper body. In that instant, I missed the feeling of his strong hands on my body, and hated that I'd spent recent hours in bed with Raphael.

"If I'm being shamelessly honest, I want you to scoop me up and take me to bed and fuck me until I can't walk," I told him.

Soren tried to play it cool, but ended up laughing, and nervously stroking his beard and rubbing the back of his neck.

I continued, "But I have a few things to handle first—and I wasn't sure if me being a vampire was a deal breaker for us."

Soren stepped in close to me, and I thought he was going to kiss me or touch me, but he didn't. "You've taught this old Viking a lot of things: like the fact that not all vampires are bad. And if you told Billy you had a good reason for turning, then you did. So go take care of your business, and get back here so I can carry you into that house and fuck you senseless."

"Yes, sir," I smiled, and turned to start back toward the Quarter. "Oh," I paused, turning back to him and trying to look very innocent and apologetic, "I think I lost my shovel and flashlight when I went into Hell."

"Hmm," Soren grunted. "Well then, you will have to be punished." He stared at me without even a smirk.

His words and the sound of his voice ran straight to things low in my body, and I was more than ready to hurry back here.

But first, back to the Quarter.

CHAPTER TWENTY-SEVEN

Everyone was back now, vampires included... well, everyone except for Grace. I was betting she was still at the boutique, or out with Melinoe. Maybe once my drama was finished, I could worry more about her choices.

Andreas and Boude had filled Ray in on my change, and how it had come to be.

Ray came up and hugged me, and said exactly what I needed to hear. "You made a good choice, Hel. I know it was a hard decision, and I'm proud of you for doing what you felt was right."

Tears stung my eyes as I tried to keep my composure. "You don't think less of me for giving up my soul? You don't think I'm damned, or something?" I didn't even know I was so worried about these things until I heard myself asking him.

His eyes were so kind and full of sincerity. He kissed me on the forehead and pulled me into a hug. "You will always be my little girl. I will never believe you could be damned or damaged. I couldn't be prouder of you."

I thought of all the things he taught me through

the years, and how good he had been to me. He'd never raised his voice or acted like I had been a disappointment in any way. He never resented choosing to be my "dad." I might have been Loki's daughter, but Ray was my dad—and for all the misery I had been through, I'd have done it again.

"I love you so much, and I'm so happy you're here," I said with my face still buried against his shirt.

"I love you too," he said, and pulled back so that we would be at an appropriate distance to talk.

"I got to talk to someone at the Assignment Hall," he said.

I dried my eyes and said, "Oh? What did they say?"

"Well, you know I was in process to be reincarnated when that door opened up."

Fear made my shoulders tighten. "Are they sending you back?"

"I didn't have anything in my file against me, so they agreed that I could stay here if I wanted, and take on a job," he said.

I was getting anxious, and wanted him to get to the point. "Are you going to? Will you stay?" I asked.

"Part of me wants to experience everything I can, alive or dead. So I asked if I could stay a while, and go on to my next life whenever I'm ready…" he paused again, "and they said I could! So I hope you don't mind having me around a while," he grinned.

Relief washed over me, and I playfully slapped him on the shoulder. "Don't scare me like that! So what job are you taking on? Do you want to be a reaper?" I asked him.

Ray put his hands in his pockets and smiled while shaking his head. "No, I think I had my fill of digging in the dirt while I was alive. I told them I'd run one of the little shops in town—a furniture place I think it was. I've never done anything like that before."

I smiled at him. I loved that he still wanted to do new things and gain knowledge. Me? I'd probably be happy digging forever, on one side of the grave or the other.

"Yes, yes, this is all very heart-warming, but is everything back to normal now? Can I please go back to my own place, and *stay* there?" Andreas asked, in his oh-so-special way.

"Yes, Andreas, you can go home: all of us can," I told him.

Boude nodded in understanding. "Are you out of your soul contract, so to speak?"

I smiled, "I am."

"Bravo!" Andreas cheered. "It worked out well for you and me, since now I don't have to listen to you go on and on about how 'precious' souls are."

I rolled my eyes at him. "I am still grateful to you and Boude for turning me."

Boude gave a gracious bow, and Andreas looked entirely too pleased with himself.

Raphael had been quiet through all of this. It was Ray who finally turned to him and asked, "What did they tell you at the Assignment Hall?"

"They apologized for the mistake of me getting abandoned in Hell, so I'm free to choose any job, living quarters, or other afterlife that I want to go to," he said, but he didn't sound happy about it.

"So what will you choose?" Boude asked.

Raphael answered Boude, but looked at me. "I'm not sure yet."

We both knew a talk was imminent.

Ray sensed the tension in the room and interjected, "My job comes with a nice apartment right above it! I get a good view of everything."

"That's great," we all told him.

"Well then, since we are no longer in the throes of a crisis, I am going home. I will see all of you… at some point." His suitcases were packed and waiting by the door. To be such a vibrant character, Andreas certainly needed a lot of alone-time.

Boude looked around at everyone. "I wouldn't mind taking off as well. Does anyone need anything before I go?"

When no one said anything, Boude went to collect his things and left as well.

"It feels weird here with fewer people," I said.

"I agree. Big houses just aren't meant to be empty," Ray said. "Let's get our things and head back into town. I'm sure I can go ahead and take the apartment, and you two can stay with me if you need to."

I knew staying with Ray was not my plan for us, but I didn't want to be here any longer either. "Sure, we can head back."

None of us had much to take, but I did get the few snacks we had left to take home or give to Ray. No sense in it going to waste. *Does food here even spoil?* I hadn't thought about it before.

Raphael and I walked Ray to his apartment, and we all agreed it was a nice place in a pretty part of the city. We left him to get settled and told him we'd check on him later.

I was so happy he was staying my heart could just burst. And then, looking at Raphael and wondering if

I was about to break his heart, hurt mine. *Can a heart be that happy, and that broken at the same time?*

Raphael let me lead as we weaved up and down the streets. I stopped when we came to the fountain in the square. I sat down on the edge of the fountain and let my fingers play in the water.

The fountain wasn't intimidating to me anymore; it was just water and metal. The sun wasn't shining, so it's magical properties weren't active.

Raphael sat next to me, and I told him about the fountain: how it was the only place in the underworld where you could check on the living, but only when the sun was shining, which was a very rare occurrence. I told him about me rushing to get here the first time I saw the sun, just so I could get a glimpse of him. I told him how devastated I had been over what I saw.

He took my hand in his, and I said, "Raphael, I have never felt love for anyone like the love I felt for you. For the short time we knew each other, for me to fall that hard and be that obsessed—it was insane."

"I guess now that you know it wasn't your own feelings about me, it makes more sense," he said.

"I don't believe it was all a trick. I can't believe that I could be that deeply fooled. I am forever happy that I felt that way over you. I don't think many people ever experience love on that level. I'm just sorry you were dragged into my mess."

He didn't reply.

"Did you love me like that? Was it an all-consuming, can't-breathe-without-me kind of love?" I asked because I was genuinely curious.

"You intrigued me. You were unlike any woman I had ever met, and I did find myself falling for you pretty quickly. I had experienced so much death and loss; I was lonely, and trying to find ways to cope, and you were the first person to make me OK after all of that," he told me.

I smiled. "I'm glad I could do that for you. It wasn't the same though, was it? You didn't have the same ache for me that I did for you. You weren't madly in love with me."

"No," he answered. "But when you were killed, I fell into a horrible place. I believed that I was cursed, and that anyone I cared for was going to die or leave me."

"I could understand that," I agreed.

He went on, "And then I didn't know what I was doing after I died, or where I was supposed to be. When you showed up in Hell, I just couldn't believe it, and the fact that you had missed me, and came specifically to save me…" he touched my face, and I leaned into his palm, "that's when I fell in love with you."

"You need a fresh start," I said. "Someone who isn't always going to be somehow involved with so much death. My destiny might have changed, but digging graves and reaping souls is still what I want to do. I don't think you really want to be involved in that forever."

"You don't feel the same anymore, do you?" he asked.

"I understand why I did at the time, but I've changed a lot—and I don't want you to love me just because I saved you. You deserve so much more than that." An idea came to me. "Go to the Assignment Hall and ask Margaret to look up the file of your friend, Stephanie. Maybe you can find her!"

"I can do that?" Raphael asked.

"It might not work, but you can ask," I urged.

Hope sparked in his so-blue eyes, and I wished with everything in me that he found her.

We both stood up, and he hugged me. "I guess this is it," he said.

"If you leave this underworld, you better come say goodbye," I ordered.

"Of course," he said.

I watched him walk away, and tried not to let myself feel too much about all of it, because I didn't know what I was supposed to feel. I just tried to picture him happy.

CHAPTER TWENTY-EIGHT

THE LAST THING I HAD TO TAKE CARE OF BEFORE getting back to the fields of dead was stopping in the shop to see Grace. It seemed like so much had happened since I had been turned, I couldn't believe I hadn't filled her in.

I walked up behind her as she was hanging a shirt back on a rack, and surprised her.

She immediately burst into tears, and wrapped her arms around me. "Andreas told me you were fine after I got Boude, but I saw you almost die!"

"I'm fine! Thank you for getting Boude for us. I'm sure that was difficult," I told her.

She waved her hand like it was no big deal, but I knew it must've been awkward.

"So what all has happened since then?" Grace asked me.

"A lot. We need hours to catch up, but the big things are that Raphael and I didn't work out, I don't have to rule the underworld, and I'm going home to Soren and the fields. Oh, and Ray is staying," I smiled.

Grace looked at me in disbelief. "Too much. Like, I can't even begin to process some of what you said.

It's all good, though, right? We're happy about all of this?"

"Yes. It's still a lot for me to process myself, but we're happy. How are things with you and Melinoe?"

Grace adjusted the red bandana she had in her hair, and straightened her eye patch in the dressing room mirror. She let out a breath. "She's intense, and dark, and so much fun."

"Are we happy?" I asked her.

"Yes... I mean I don't know what's happening between us, but right now it's exciting, and very good," Grace said.

"Good. Come by sometime soon and we'll go hunting together," I suggested.

Grace actually jumped up and down and clapped her hands together like a little kid. "YES!" she squealed. "That would be amazing."

I hugged her again, and headed towards the fields.

As the brown dirt and gray sky met in the most boring horizon ever, I was giddy to get back to what I loved: my friends, my work, simple days of digging in the dirt and helping souls move forward.

Soren saw me walking towards him, and smiled at me. He scooped me up, just like he had promised, and carried me towards my house.

"Everything is just like you left it," he told me as he opened the door.

I didn't know if Soren was my forever person—forever could change on a dime. He was my right now person, and maybe that was even better, because I understood how easily all of this could disappear.

His steel gray eyes looked into mine as he laid me on the bed and kissed me. *I almost missed this—almost let it all slip through my fingers.*

To Hell with destiny, I was doing things my way.

THE STORY WILL CONTINUE...

Want to be the first to have a sneak peek at my new books, giveaways, and free Kindle downloads?

JOIN MY MAILING LIST!

https://mailchi.mp/fa5e03851766/williedalton

ABOUT THE AUTHOR

WILLIE E. DALTON is a full-time writer at her home in Duffield, Va. She is the author of *Three Witches in a Small Town*, *The Dark Side of the Woods*, and *The Gravedigger series*. When she is isn't writing, Willie is an active volunteer for the local cat rescue "Appalachian Feline Friends."

To learn more about Willie and her books, go to:
WWW.AUTHORWILLIEDALTON.COM
WWW.FACEBOOK.COM/THREEWITCHESINASMALLTOWN
WWW.INSTAGRAM.COM/AUTHORWILLIEDALTON
WWW.AUTHORWILLIEDALTON.COM

www.ingramcontent.com/pod-product-compliance
Lightning Source LLC
LaVergne TN
LVHW041634060526
838200LV00040B/1563